the Gift

Ancient Secrets
of Solomon's Wisdom

Jeffery Mitchell

E\/ergreen
PRESS

Mobile, Alabama

The Gift
by Jeff Mitchell
Copyright ©2012 Jeff Mitchell

Unless otherwise identified, Scripture quotations are taken from *THE HOLY BIBLE: New International Version* ©1984 by the New York International Bible Society, used by permission of Zondervan Bible Publishers.

Scriptures marked NASB are taken from the *New American Standard Bible*, Copyright ©1960, 1962, 1963, 1968, 1971, 1973, 1975, 1977 by The Lockman Foundation.

ISBN 978-1-58169-381-2
For Worldwide Distribution
Printed in the U.S.A.

Evergreen Press
P.O. Box 191540 • Mobile, AL 36619
800-367-8203

"A story is a letter the author writes to himself
to tell himself things that he would be
unable to discover otherwise."
—Carlos Ruiz Zafon

For Gael, Cara Mia—
Thank you for encouraging me
to write my letter

In memory of my father,
Robert Walter Mitchell
1928-2011

Acknowledgments

I am grateful to my parents for their support and love. Mom and Dad raised me to travel; and my brother, Steve, taught me the joy of living and telling a story.

My own family has faithfully and silently allowed me the grace to steal away to my writing place. I hope this has been worth the wait. Emily and Monica, your honorable lives and beautiful families bless and fill me with peace.

My church family—Good Samaritan—has enabled me to know the truth about congregational life, and its hope and pain is setting me free. I am indebted to the Monday morning men's Bible study for letting me think and learn out loud. It's rare to find such places these days. There are many of you at Good Sam who walk with me and let me walk with you. I am tempted to name you, but you know who you are. I will make one exception. Wendy Johnson bravely said yes to helping me with this project a few years ago—thank you.

I have a wonderful family in the spiritual direction community. The Pacific Southwest Conference of Pastoral Spiritual Directors first took me in like a baby left on their doorstep. The Bread of Life Center for Spiritual Formation mentors and interns introduced me to what my heart was longing for. My director, supervisor, and directees stir that longing every time we sit together.

A family of writers, encouragers, and truth tellers have also gathered around me and this project: Tom Eisenman, Cathy Barsotti, Barb Holland, Wayne Jacobsen, Rob Johnston, and Sandra Lommasson. Jeff Banashak, his family, and the team at Evergreen Press have been so patiently helpful and willing to share this endeavor and bring it to life. I am thankful for each of these.

I want to acknowledge the Lilly Endowment Clergy Renewal Program whose grant financed our sabbatical. Thanks to Jim Sundholm, former director of Covenant World Relief for introducing and leading me to Ethiopia, where this story began.

Finally I am joyfully indebted to Bruce Baloian who planted the first spiritual seed in my heart. You watered that seed with the King David stories. Thanks, Bruce.

Dear Reader,

The story you are about to read was inspired by our experience in Ethiopia while on sabbatical. Gael and I had the rare privilege of meeting the people and visiting the locations mentioned in this book.

The discovery and existence of the Book of Zadok is pure fiction. However, the story remains faithful to the biblical Solomon, containing wisdom that is true and potentially life-changing.

Please enjoy the book. May it touch your heart.

Blessings,
Jeff Mitchell

ETHIOPIA

Present Day

Chapter I

eaving the holy city of Axum, we enter the vast mountainous desert of East Africa's horn. We are headed due east on a dirt track riddled with potholes. The early morning sun rises over the spectacular Adwa Mountains, ascending into a yellow sky accented with stubborn clouds that refuse to rain. The drought stricken earth had turned to dust, a silky powder everywhere. The stench of human sweat, stale tobacco, and gasoline foul the interior of our early model Land Cruiser. An occasional hint of sage from the sparse but obstinate shrub provides some aromatic relief.

Our driver, Misganu, is a pleasant young man who speaks no English, and we speak no Amharic. So we all exchange smiles and point a lot. Takelte, our guide for the day, is a ten-year-old boy who humbles us with his fluency in both languages. He is the house boy of our main guide, Haile, and is very excited to be our guide-in-training. We are overjoyed at any and all help that comes our way on this wild adventure.

Our journey began roughly eight weeks earlier. My wife, Gael, and I were invited to teach in the western town of Nekemte. Gael taught in a children's school for the deaf, and I at a small Bible college. Our journey to Ethiopia is part of a sabbatical. Upon completing our teaching assignments, we embarked on a pilgrimage of Ethiopia's ancient Christian sites known as the Northern Historical Circuit.

Our first stop along the way was Lalibela, known as the eighth wonder of the world. Visiting Lalibela, we entered a place where time stands still. Perched precariously high in the Wollo Mountains at nearly 9,600 feet, Lalibela is an isolated refuge deserving its reputation as the "Tibet of Christianity." The crown jewel of Lalibela (if not all of Ethiopia) is the network of twelve stone-carved churches cut out of volcanic rock some eight hundred years earlier. The wonder of this site is the sheer accomplishment of the task, let alone being constructed during medieval times.

The mystery of this sacred enclave expands as one wanders among the churches, realizing they are all interconnected through a vast network of tunnels, trenches, and trails. Legend has it that construction was aided by the miraculous intervention of angels. This theory gains enhanced plausibility when one's in the presence of these massive and beautifully detailed churches.

While in Lalibela, Gael and I were introduced to the ancient customs of the Ethiopian church. We learned how to enter the church—by approaching the altar set before the Holy of Holies and receive the blessing of the priest, who held an ornate cross. These experiences enriched our visit and personalized its meaning. As we adjusted to the mysterious ways of the church, we felt less like tourists and more like pilgrims.

Our second stop was the holy city of Axum, purportedly the final resting place of ancient Israel's Ark of the Covenant. According to tradition, the link between Israel and Ethiopia (via the Ark of the Covenant) began in the biblical meeting of King Solomon and Queen Makeda of Sheba (now known as Ethiopia). Gael and I were fascinated by this rich and fanciful story that was added to and embroidered upon by those we met along our sojourn. This endearing tale of royalty seemed to spread out before us like the fine ornate tapestries and tablecloths we so admired in the village markets.

When we arrived in Axum, our guide, Haile, informed us of an extremely rare opportunity. The Ark of the Covenant was to be marched around the city in an early morning prayer procession. We were invited to participate and discovered later that the true holy Ark is never brought out, but a ceremonial replica is used in its stead. We were thrilled at the opportunity to join the vigil that began, as promised, just before daybreak. We were swept up in the spiritual current of thousands of worshipers who were dressed in robes of white gauze and held candles, torches, and incense while walking around the city in prayer, chant, and song.

Leading the procession was a man bearing a tapestry covered box on his head that was roughly the size of its biblical description. Experiencing the sights and sounds of that predawn procession, we felt as though we were transported somehow to a different time and place. It was as if we had walked into the pages of the Old Testament itself, perhaps even the high holy days when King Solomon paraded the Ark of the Covenant into the newly completed temple. It was, in every sense of the word, awesome!

Later that afternoon, we were quite surprised to receive yet another unexpected invitation, an audience with the Atang, the guardian of the Ark. Selected at the age of four, young boys are raised in the monastery in hopes of being appointed Atang. Very few westerners are given an opportunity to meet with the Atang, a most influential holy man, who is second only to the patriarch of the entire Ethiopian Orthodox Church.

Haile told us we were given an appointment to meet Abba MeKonen, the current Atang, because he had observed our respectful participation in the vigil. The Atang wanted to speak to and pray for us. We were excited to share with him about our work in Ethiopia, our pilgrimage, and our interest in King Solomon and the Ark.

When we arrived for our appointment, we were taken to the back door of the sanctuary that houses the Ark. The monks were busy displaying fine artifacts from the sanctuary's treasury. We saw the golden bejeweled crowns of the ancient kings and queens of Ethiopia. They showed us many antiquated paintings and books.

Finally, the Atang himself appeared. Abba MeKonen looked

mature not old, ordinary rather than stately, and above all noble. We could see and feel the peace of his presence. He set us at ease, like watching a harvest moon rise over the hills back home. Through an interpreter he welcomed us with warmth and sincerity. We were grateful to share in this unique moment and willingly offered the Atang our humility and respect.

When the opportunity seemed appropriate, I broached the subject of my interest, the Ark of the Covenant.

"May I ask a question?"

"It is possible," he replied.

"I have read about the meeting of King Solomon of Israel and Queen Makeda of Ethiopia in the Bible. What I don't understand is how the Ark of the Covenant came to be here in Axum."

The Atang was silent for longer than was comfortable for me. I feared my question might have been offensive in some way, ruining this wonderful occasion. Then he lifted his hand and began to speak.

"Our tradition is informed by our ancient book the *Kebre Negest,* or *Glory of the Kings*. It guides our understanding of the holy Ark, as well as other matters of great importance. It is written in Ge'ez, the first written language in all of Africa."

The holy man spoke these words with just the hint of a smile on his face, like a flower about to bloom. His pride was in proportion to the importance of this major achievement for the whole of Africa.

The Atang continued, "For now, time prevents me from giving but a shadow of the answer you seek. The *Kebre Negest* continues the story after our queen's visit to the holy city of Jerusalem. When Queen Makeda returned, she carried within her a gift beyond all other gifts—King Solomon's child. When the boy child was born, he was given the name Menelik, or son of the king. When Menelik came of age, he repeated his mother's pilgrimage to Jerusalem and the court of his father, where they would meet for the first time. King Solomon recognized and welcomed his son. Menelik remained in Jerusalem a number of years, learning the ways of Israel and the wisdom of his father. When Menelik told Solomon of his decision to return to Ethiopia, King Solomon offered him the throne of Israel, but he would not be dissuaded. Many officials and holy ones of Israel went to Ethiopia with Menelik.

"One such priest, Azariah, son of the high priest in Jerusalem, was told in a dream to take the Ark to Ethiopia for its own safe keeping; and so he did. Menelik became very angry when he discovered his entourage had taken the most holy relic, and King Solomon felt betrayed at this ungrateful act. However, Menelik and Solomon received God's word in dreams concerning the blessed Ark's movement. Menelik was welcomed home triumphantly with much rejoicing, while King Solomon kept the secret."

The Atang finished his story with a commentary. "With the unforeseen fall of Solomon's dynasty, the rise of evil kings, and the exile of Israel, we have been humble yet faithful custodians of the holy Ark, to the glory of God, ever since."

He ended his answer to my question with such authority, it felt as though nothing more should be said. I could tell right then and there that this was not the time for debate or further interrogation. Rather, it was an opportunity to honor another's tradition and contemplate this story's meaning.

I looked up and realized that the Atang was standing in silence, eyes closed. A hush was over all of us as if holding the day, the story, and one another in its silence. It was truly a beautiful and holy moment. Before long, the Atang opened his eyes and looked our way as if to invite any final questions. I had one last question, but I hesitated, struggling with whether I should ask it. Again our eyes met and I summoned the courage. I heard myself in a halting voice ask, "May I see the Ark?"

The Atang's wise response caught me off guard. "Are you able to behold the face of God?"

When put that way, I reconsidered and gracefully withdrew my request. At the close of our time together, the Atang motioned for

Gael and me to draw close. He had something special for each of us. Taking water from the sanctuary of the Ark and anointing Gael's knees, he said, "May you walk long in the land with your children and your children's children."

Then he turned to me with conviction in his voice and authority in his eyes and said, "You must go to the holy mountain." Noting the confused look on my face he continued, "You must go to a most ancient place, our oldest monastery, Debre Damo, in the east."

So after many hours driving east into the desert, the Land Cruiser skids to an abrupt stop. Having become accustomed to the bone jarring ride, being still feels strange. Like stepping onto firm land from a rocky boat, it seems as if we should still be moving. The driver excitedly points in the direction of the *ambo*, a huge flat topped mountain on the horizon. Takelte translates, "Debre Damo is on that plateau."

If I considered the last four hours of driving impossible, the next hour is simply insane. We leave the main road for the desert outback. At times the road is indiscernible to me. Misganu is thrilled, hands firmly on the controls like a fighter pilot. He flashes me a huge smile, his mouth starved for teeth, as if to say, "Just think, you pay me to do this!" Up and over hills and sand dunes we fly, clearing most of the big rocks but few of the bushes. He cuts down the shrubs like the enemy of a fantasy dogfight, currently high over the desert of Ethiopia. I hold on and pray for a safe landing.

Pausing at the edge of a river bed, we drive the Cruiser down into the gulley, building momentum, so we can successfully cross the sandy bottom and make it up the other side. Negotiating this obstacle, Misganu and Takelte are giving each other high fives, rejoicing over Misganu's success on the first try.

Takelte confides, "If there is a flash flood, we could be stuck in the desert on the wrong side of the river for a week."

I pray for continued drought.

We drive as close to the mountain as the Cruiser will take us. Misganu points to the rocky cliff before us, and we all stiffly get out and stretch before we begin our trek towards it. With the exuberance of youth, Takelte takes off and encourages us to follow. As I follow, I realize something looks odd about the entrance to the monastery. The doorway appears to be about one hundred feet above the ground, and I can see no way up—no stairs, no ladder, nothing. The closer I get, I see what appears to be a long, skinny piece of knotted rawhide hanging down the cliff to the ground. Before I can comprehend the task ahead of me, Takelte is already halfway up the "rope." A moment later I hear him yelling from the top, "Pastor Jeff, come up . . . Pastor Jeff, climb the rope. God is with you, Pastor Jeff!"

CHAPTER II

efore I decide to follow young Takelte to the monastery, we are informed that no women are allowed beyond this point. Gael decides to go in search of the nunnery that we are told is somewhere around the mountain base. This option proves uneventful. Soon she is settled with lunch and a place to rest in a local hut turned tea house for ill-prepared pilgrims. I give her my reassurance that I will be fine but caution her that I do not know how long I will be. Somehow I sense that this is going to take awhile.

I resolutely turn toward the daunting eighty-foot climb to the top. It would be a challenge, but I've come all this way, so I decide to go for it. After climbing high enough to be really scared, fear propels me the rest of the way. As I struggle, I can hear what sound like encouraging words coming from the top. Once there, I'm met by friendly monks who pull me to safety across the cliffside threshold. Grateful to be on solid ground once again, I am greeted with surprised congratulations and hugs all around. In their celebration they confess their skepticism at my ability to perform the task. Their genuine excitement is founded in the relief and pride of having encouraged me to risk the impossible. I take all this in stride, yet shudder at my first peek over the side of the cliff. I refuse to think about how I'm going to get down.

My young translator leads the way up the ascending path toward the summit. On top, the wide expanse reveals a labyrinth of rooms and prayer cells, housing as many as three hundred monks and priests, or so Takelte proudly tells me. From the center of the complex, a bell tower rises into the sky. The 360-degree view from the tower is impressive. Beyond the ancient monastery itself, we are able to see the horizon everywhere we look. From our perch, it seems as if we're at the top of the world while the earth appears to drop off in all directions.

In the windblown silence of that place, I feel that I might be standing on some kind of high pinnacle in my life inquiring, *Is this the place I step off and fly?* I have the impression of being in the presence of something larger than myself that is calling out to me. Whatever it is or would become is unfolding before me. My silent moment is suddenly broken by ravens screeching overhead.

We make our way towards the main church, which I learn is the oldest in Ethiopia. Observing several monks in their prayer cells, we are motioned to join them for a visit. Their space is sparse but full of joy. Being drawn toward the church, we do not interrupt their prayer for long. As I approach, I can feel the antiquity I see. The external walls are sturdy, fashioned with thick layers of rough cut lumber and whitewashed stone.

We remove our shoes to enter the sanctuary, which is fully carpeted with layers of deep, colorful handmade rugs. The ceiling is made of wood panels, each one decorated with beautifully carved animals. As I immerse myself in the wonder of this place, the Abba walks out from behind the Holy of Holies to greet us.

Raising his arms, he greets us: "Welcome in the name of the Lord Jesus!"

He too is impressive, extravagantly robed, carrying his prayer staff and blessing cross, and I am pleasantly surprised to hear him speaking English. I receive his greeting with a slight bow of my head and introduce myself.

Awestruck by the moment, I could think of nothing else to add except the obvious question, "How did all of this get here?"

The Abba smiles and then begins to tell the story. "In the early days of Christianity here in Ethiopia, nine saints were led to this wilderness to inhabit its silence with prayer. One of these saints, Abuna Aragani, came to the foot of this curious, flat-topped mountain. He realized that the plateau was perfectly suited for the solitary life he craved. God delighted in the desire of the saint's heart and called upon a flying serpent to carry Abuna Aragani to the summit where he founded Debre Damo."

My unspoken response is, *And I thought the rope was an adventure!*

After pausing to consider the story, the Abba continues, "Pastor Jeff, may I ask you a question?"

"Sure," I reply.

"Why have you come to our sanctuary? You have come from a great distance, no?"

"I have indeed." I explain my sabbatical activities, my need for rest, and my interest in King Solomon, the Ark of the Covenant, and ancient Christianity.

The Abba considers this for a moment and then continues, "But *why* are you here, my friend? What is the desire of your heart?"

This question is more difficult, uncomfortable, even intrusive. I notice my resistance is rising, and I'm thinking, *I'd rather be a tourist now instead of a pilgrim.* As I consider the Abba's question, I ask myself, *Why did I come here?* After a brief pause, I figure I've already taken a risk with my life on that rope, why not risk my heart and be honest.

I begin, "I'm not really sure why I'm here; I guess I'd like to know myself better. I wonder at times why I work so hard to gain the approval of others, why I strive so diligently to prove myself in my own eyes and in the eyes of my peers."

The wise Abba patiently listens; I can feel him holding our conversation in his heart.

"You wish to know yourself?" he repeats.

"Yes," I hear myself say, my confidence growing. "I think I've been so busy with everyone and everything else, I'm not sure I know who I am anymore. I wonder if I have ever really known who I am." As I'm saying these words, I notice that feeling again, the feeling from the bell tower, like something is happening to me or in me that could change the course of my life forever.

The Abba asks, "Pastor Jeff, do you have time for me to read you a story?"

I consider the request with all the things I had begun to feel and think, and simply surrender to his request. "Yes, I'd love to hear a story."

The Abba goes behind the Holy of Holies and retrieves an ancient manuscript. It is like so many we had already seen, a primitive book written in Ge'ez. We sit together on the soft carpet of that quiet sanctuary, on the top of a mountain in the center of the world, in the middle of nowhere. Time is not an issue; we have no agenda or interruptions. The Abba and I are the only ones here, and the ever increasing presence of God is calling, leading, and speaking to us in this holy space.

Before reading, the Abba provides a brief introduction. "This is a very old book, maybe the oldest book we have. It is called the Book of Zadok. It tells the story of the very heart of King Solomon. I will translate for you as I read."

He bows his head in silent prayer before opening the book, then proceeds to read the book written so many centuries before by Zadok.

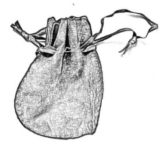

THE
BOOK OF ZADOK
PART 1

Jerusalem 970 BC

CHAPTER III

I n the first year of King Solomon's reign, the third king of Israel and son of the great King David, I awoke to an unexpected knocking at my door in the middle of the night. "Zadok," commanded a voice, "prepare to enter the presence and service of your king."

I am Zadok, the High Priest of King Solomon, and this is my eyewitness account that you now incline your ears to hear. Serving both King David and King Solomon has filled my heart with important stories, insights, and wisdom as yet known to only a very few.

Dear ones, I encourage you that this tale contains life-giving truth. Be forewarned, its mysteries and wonders can be stubborn. Like most genuine virtues, they give up their treasures reluctantly. Therefore, attend to what you hear! Receive and live the wisdom herein. So now the story begins. Carefully listen to it...

<hr />

I was startled by the rapping at my door and the announcement. Before I was fully awake, I realized I was being led to the king's chamber. Until this very night my relationship to the king had been limited to my formal priestly and ceremonial duties. This was all about to change. As I entered my Lord's chambers, I was in the presence of a king who was completely undone and seemingly at his wits' end. Gone was the powerful, confident young king in charge. Solomon now appeared as a very troubled man, burdened with his concerns, fears, and responsibilities. It occurred to me that few had seen this side of the new king; I surely had not. He appeared sorely in need of a listening friend, someone who could hear his thoughts, feel his pain, and look with compassion at the man within the stone-chiseled public image.

My thoughts were interrupted as I realized the king was speaking to me. "I am not sure how to begin this conversation," said the king, full of hesitation. "I know not what to do. I know I need something but am not sure what it is. As my priest, might you be able to help me?"

Feeling my own uncertainty I responded, "What seems to be troubling you?"

"Well, I am often visited by a terrible dream in which I find myself running in panic from room to room, seeking a way out. I try a number of doors and windows, but none leads to an exit. I feel driven to get out, panicked with the terror of being closed in forever. Exhausted by my desperate but futile search, I am relieved to wake up, drenched in sweat with a racing heart."

"It sounds as if you feel trapped by your life. What can you tell me about that?" I inquired.

"I have struggled tremendously beneath the burden of this kingdom," he began. "I know not whether I am able to do this, or whether I even desire it. Receiving power was easy; managing and holding on to it is terrifying for me. I must constantly be on guard, looking over my shoulder, watching my back for anyone who seeks to do me harm and seize my authority. At times I simply do not know whom I can trust. I am not even sure I can trust you, but I am desperately in need of help.

"I will admit that the fresh feeling of power was surprisingly intoxicating at first. I thought I could do whatever I wanted, with nothing in my way. In public, I have played the part with a brave, unflinching face—full of swagger and authority. However, behind closed doors I am living in fear, crippled by my suspicion of others and their intentions. In fact, struggling to hold power in my kingdom leaves me very little time to rule over its daily demands. The privilege of being king is outweighed by its frightful responsibility." The king gave a long sigh.

I was beginning to understand why the Solomon before me was so different from the king I had seen only from a distance. So I asked another question. "What have you been doing since you became king?"

"I did what I had to do; I began the distasteful work of establishing my kingdom. Surely you've noticed my strategies and movements. I had my half brother, Adonijah, killed, eliminating his threat to my throne and family. I also had Joab—that untrustworthy and blood-soaked commander—killed along with a number of my father's other 'friends' and enemies. I replaced the unfaithful priest Abiathar with you, although I did spare his life. Beyond our kingdom, I've felt politically vulnerable with Egypt to the south. Therefore, I forged a peace alliance by marrying Pharaoh's daughter."

The king sat in silence as if considering his list of unsavory deeds. I studied the king. I could now understand as well as sense his concerns. After a moment I asked, "How does all this feel?"

"I am unsure," was Solomon's reply. "On the one hand I am surviving; this is what one does when one becomes king. I do the dirty work of the kingdom. I judge, condemn, kill, plot, manipulate, and compromise. I am the king and I must rule. On the other hand, I do not like what I have done or am doing. My once innocent and naïve heart is dark as coal and twice as hard. Fear and dread are what I feel. I am discovering that this is a very cruel, kill-or-be-killed world. Now my own conscience accuses me of being no better than those whom I have judged, and I believe those charges to be true. Consequently I am frustrated, exhausted, and discouraged in my short reign as king. So it seems the great kingdom of Israel is shrinking in my own eyes and has become as meaningless as its failing young king. I fear that my hope is fading."

"What is your hope, O King?"

"I once believed that my mother's protection and love were enough to give me hope for the future. However, it appears that her handfed, sheltered upbringing only fueled my naïveté that life and rule should be effortless once I came to power as king. Now I realize this was merely a loving mother's dream for her son. This surely was not the hope that could enable me to lead a lord's life in this kingdom.

"I have attempted to follow in the footsteps of my father, the warrior, but this has proved hopeless as well. The great King David ruled with a fist of iron. I must admit my hands are soft with royal pampering, not calloused for handling power. I cannot exercise my will on the kingdom and make it follow my demands. Even when I use my power as king, the results do not satisfy me, as you are beginning to see. I am not my father and fear I am not much of a king.

"I have recalled my father's spiritual and reflective way, considering this might be my hope. I remembered a song from my childhood that my father would often sing. It was a song about the source of his hope.

> *Search me, O God, and know my heart;*
> *Try me and know my anxious thoughts;*
> *And see if there be any hurtful way in me,*
> *And lead me in the everlasting way.[i]*

"Pondering the words to that song as an adult, I realized I had never thought of asking God for help. In fact, I had never asked anything of God for that matter. Everything in life had always been handed to me—even this kingdom. I have wanted for absolutely nothing my entire life, until now. Now I need help. This kingdom is too much for me; I truly need the help of God. I cannot eat, sleep, or think. It feels as though I have a terrible disease. My body seems overrun as if fighting for its life. But it is more than physical, you see; I feel an all-encompassing soul sickness that is bent on my destruction. In my heart I am so deeply troubled. I cannot go on like this . . ."

"And what about the hope and presence of the Lord God?" I inquired.

"I have come to the conclusion that this is at the very root of my soul's illness and turmoil. I have sought the Lord with great expectation, only to be left abandoned and hopeless once again."

"How, O King, has this come to be?"

"In my desperation for help, I determined to make a secret pilgrimage to the high holy place at Mt. Gibeon and seek the Lord's presence."

"And what happened? Did you find the Lord there?

"I did, but as you can see it has turned out to be meaningless. My hopes are dashed and I am more confused than ever. I—"

Thoughtlessly, I interrupted the king. "But I need—rather want to hear the story of your pilgrimage." The king sat in silence, his mouth shut tight, sprung like a fowler's trap.

Just as I had resigned myself to the abrupt close of our conversation, the king remarked, "I will tell you more soon. I have called on you for help, if such a thing is possible. I am grateful you have come in my time of need as a faithful priest. But now is not the time for a long story, not tonight. I am so weary of my situation and this conversation. Fatigue overwhelms me, but thank you just the same for your kind presence."

CHAPTER IV

 few days later I found myself sitting before the king, listening as he shared about his pilgrimage to Mt. Gibeon. The king began, "The trek north was uneventful, but it took the whole day to move our company from Jerusalem to the foot of the high place. We made camp as darkness overtook us. The night was cool on the high plateau of the Judean hills; the skies were peaceful, filled with abundant stars, yet my sleep was restless as I anticipated the next day.

"At first light I arose to stunning views in every direction I set my eyes. Before me into the west was my destination, the high place of sacrifice. Behind me to the east was the Jordan River Valley. I am told this huge basin cuts a massive, earthen scar across the world, stretching forth from Galilee in the north, south into Midian of the Patriarchs, deep into the Gulf of Aqaba, and beyond the land of Cush where the great Queen of Sheba holds court in Axum. Directly across from us, the sun was rising like pure gold from its crucible, Mt. Nebo, where Moses received his only glimpse into our land of promise.

"Time stood still. I could scarcely breathe as I took in the natural and spiritual panorama. Considering my own divine appointment, I could not help but think about Moses, who spoke to God face to face as a man speaks to a friend. With the great lawgiver on my mind, I slowly began my cautious ascent to the high altar. The path before me was like the steep steps of a majestic temple leading to a summit shrouded in clouds.

"Climbing heavenward, I recalled that amazing text in the Torah where Moses, beseeching the Lord of glory, cried out in desperation, 'Now show me your glory.' The Lord's response was more startling than the request. Safe within the cleft of a rock and covered by the hand of the Divine, God allowed Moses to see merely the back side of the Lord's glory. Moses wrote of his experience as follows:

> *Then the Lord came down in the cloud and stood there with him and proclaimed his name, the Lord. And he passed in front of Moses, proclaiming, "The Lord, the Lord, the compassionate and gracious God, slow to anger, abounding in love and faithfulness, maintaining love to thousands, and forgiving wickedness, rebellion and sin."[ii]*

"I considered my own destiny stretched out before me on the trail that morning. Would God receive me and my sacrifice? What would God say to me? What would I say to God? There was no way to answer the flood of questions and anxieties filling my heart and mind. I knew not what to expect, what I was doing, or what I would do. However, it dawned on me that I was offering no mere sacrifice; I was offering myself, whatever that meant, unsure I would leave the mountain alive.

"These things were above and beyond my ability to understand. This was all too great for me to comprehend. A sense of humility and reverence came upon me. Jarred from my thoughts, I could see I was within steps of the bronze altar crafted by Bezalele in the days of Moses. We sacrificed one thousand burnt offerings that day before the Lord, and at sunset the Lord God appeared and spoke. 'Ask for whatever you want me to give you' was what he said to me."

I answered, "You have shown great kindness to your servant, my father, David, because he was faithful to you and righteous and upright in heart. You have continued this great kindness to him and have given him a son to sit on his throne this very day.

"Now, O Lord my God, you have made your servant king in place of my father David. But I do not know how to carry out my duties. Your servant is here among the people you have chosen, a great people, too numerous to count or number. So give your servant a discerning heart to govern your people and to distinguish between right and wrong. For who is able to govern this great people of yours?"

"God said to me, 'Since you have asked for this and not for long life or wealth for yourself, nor have asked for the death of your enemies but for discernment in administering justice, I will do what you have asked. I will give you a wise and discerning heart, so that there will never have been anyone like you, nor will there ever be. Moreover, I will give you what you have not asked for—both riches and honor—so that in your lifetime you will have no equal among kings. And if you walk in my ways and obey my statutes and commands as David your father did, I will give you a long life.'[iii]

"I returned elated, as well as perplexed. On the one hand, I sensed that the Lord was pleased with my seeking a discerning heart of wisdom and intended not only to make me wise but wealthy and powerful as well. What troubled me was the how. How was God going to do this? I recalled the Lord's words at Gibeon:

> *And if you walk in my ways and obey my statutes and commands*
> *as David your father did, I will give you long life.'[iv]*

"Once again I found myself confronted with my father's life. Who had my father really been? Why did he think, act, and speak as he did? How did he relate to others? How did he walk before the Lord and how could I follow in his footsteps? I hardly knew my father. My elation eventually dissolved into heaviness of heart. How was I to understand all of this, let alone act upon it? Why has God offered me such a glorious promise with no clue as to how to redeem it? I have felt completely abandoned by God from that day until now."

The king sat in frustrated silence. I was also greatly troubled by these things. Then I heard the king begin to inquire of me.

"You served my father, David. Perhaps you could tell me how he walked before the Lord?"

I responded, "Please, O King, give me time to consider your request and reflect on the things that could be of any help. Then we can sit together and talk of these matters."

The king agreed, and I left his chambers asking God to grant me wisdom as well in the difficult task I now faced.

CHAPTER V

I labored a few days in prayer and preparation concerning King Solomon's petition before returning to the king and continuing our conversation.

I began, "Your father, David, was a great man in every sense of the word. He was a powerful king; he eluded his enemies, won huge battles, built a formidable kingdom, and amassed a mighty fortune. However, his kingdom was not without challenge. As you well know, his leaders and even his sons sought to deceive him.

"On the one hand he was a considerable man of God. He wrote beautiful worship songs; he loved the Lord our God and together they developed a deep and intimate relationship. However, he was a man who also failed morally through lying, adultery, and even murder. These transgressions ruined much, if not all, he had gained in his life, especially in your family.

"Your father, however, had a way of recognizing his sin, confessing it, and repenting before his Creator. God forgave David's transgression and restored his heart. Listen to this, perhaps your father's crowning song:

> *Have mercy on me O God, according to your unfailing love; according to your great compassion blot out my transgressions. Wash away all my iniquity and cleanse me from my sin. For I know my transgressions, and my sin is always before me. Against you, you only, have I sinned and done what is evil in your sight, so that you are proved right when you speak and justified when you judge. Surely I was sinful at birth, sinful from the time my mother conceived me. Surely you desire truth in the inner parts; you teach me wisdom in the inmost place.*

Cleanse me with hyssop, and I will be clean; wash me, and I will be whiter than snow. Let me hear joy and gladness; let the bones you have crushed rejoice. Hide your face from my sins and blot out all my iniquity. Create in me a pure heart, O God, and renew a steadfast spirit within me.

Do not cast me from your presence or take your Holy Spirit from me. Restore to me the joy of your salvation and grant me a willing spirit to sustain me. Then I will teach transgressors your ways, and sinners will turn back to you. Save me from bloodguilt, O God, the God who saves me, and my tongue will sing of your righteousness. O Lord, open my lips, and my mouth will declare your praise. You do not delight in sacrifice, or I would bring it; you do not take pleasure in burnt offerings. The sacrifices of God are a broken spirit; a broken and contrite heart, O God, you will not despise. In your good pleasure make Zion prosper; build up the walls of Jerusalem. Then there will be righteous sacrifices, whole burnt offerings to delight you; then bulls will be offered on your altar.[v]

"Solomon, your father did many extraordinary things, both good and bad. I believe, in time, he will become known as one who understood his own heart and how to be reconciled to the heart of God. He will be remembered as the man after God's own heart."

The king could no longer restrain himself and blurted out, "But how did he do that? I know not where to start, what to say, how to think, or when to act. I feel completely lost in all this talk."

Aware of the king's deep frustration, I was patient with the outburst and waited for him to settle down.

"I do have a few questions for you that may help us find the answers you so desperately seek."

The king became attentive so I began my inquiry, "When did you last speak with your father?"

The king answered, "On the night before his death when I became king."

"What happened?" I asked.

The king replied, "It had been an unusually exciting day for me, with everything surrounding my coronation as king. That evening, my father summoned me to his chambers. I remember my thoughts being scattered. I was unsure if we would be talking king to king or father to son. We had so few conversations in my life I was not sure what to think of his mood that night. He was very sober but full of anticipation as well."

"This could be very important," I quickly replied and suggested, "take your time as you tell me everything about that night, all you were thinking and feeling."

Solomon paused, then began by saying, "As we sat down to talk, the old king, my father, began by way of confession, saying something like this: 'While I know I have given my heart to and life for the Lord our God, I have taken back much for myself—too much. It has been a life of very bright moments connected by periods of great darkness. Yet, like the caves of the desert, even in darkness, our God led me and taught me. Solomon, I have lived a double life, one that was true and false, right and wrong, selfless and selfish.

"'In my endeavor to serve the Lord and lead His kingdom, I have forsaken my own family. All of my sons, my wives, and daughters I have failed. For this, Solomon, please forgive me. I have failed you most of all. While you inherit a mighty, thriving kingdom, you will also receive its clay feet and soft underbelly. For this I am responsible and very sorry indeed. My life has been a contradiction, full of hypocrisy because of my attempt to satisfy myself. The only true peace I have ever known is being with God as a shepherd boy, as a king without a kingdom roaming the desert, on my face in the hills, pleading and praying, dancing before the Ark of the Covenant in wild worship.'"

Solomon continued, "I was emotionally overwhelmed by my father's open and honest admissions. In all my years I had never known my father. He was never anything less than the king. My father had been a powerful ruler, a mighty warrior, and a devoted follower of God. My father's solitary pursuit of this vision left little room for me and my life. At the same time, I was saddened and angry at my father's words. This confession confirmed the suspicion I had spent my whole life denying . . . In the presence of my father, I had always felt this cursed impotence that left me restless and unsure. I never knew the love of a father.

"As I peered deep into my father's eyes, I could make out my own reflection. I began to wonder at the image of myself. How could I be myself in the shadow of the one on whom my gaze was fixed? On that night, for a brief moment, I had nearly been encouraged by my father's words. But then he died, and that conversation, along with any hope, was entombed with him forever. Since then I have been condemned to follow in his footsteps, an impossible and desperate task."

I decided now was the time to broach the subject that had been heavy on my mind since Solomon had asked me for help.

"Did your father ever speak with you about the Gift? Did he try to leave something with you?" When I asked this question, Solomon's eyes widened, his mouth opening to reveal a slight expression of recognition.

"My father did say something about a gift, but he was old and close to death; his words seemed like so much nonsense at the time. So I did not give it another thought."

"What did he say?" I persisted, trying to hold in my mounting excitement.

"I recall my father repeating how he had failed and had disappointed me. He conceded that there was nothing he could do to satisfy my broken heart. I then remember him saying: 'Strange as it may seem, I must be faithful to you in at least one way. I have a Gift for you. The Gift will enable you to see yourself and others, your friends, your enemies, your beloved, and those who serve you. With this Gift you will understand and act with wisdom.'

"At the time, these words made no sense to me. Again, my father repeated himself with dire urgency: 'Solomon, Solomon, the Gift can make you see!'

"I remember he held something in his trembling, frail hands. The Gift was contained in a silk purse and secured by a drawstring. I was perplexed by the appearance and meaning of this mysterious object.

"My father set the Gift on the table before me with obvious satisfaction, as if completing an epic challenge. I became distracted from the Gift as my father turned to me to fulfill the deepest longing of my heart. 'May I now bless you, my son?' he asked. I could hardly believe my ears. I will never forget the words of his blessing spoken to me that night.

> "'I am about to go the way of all the earth,' he said. 'So be strong, show yourself a man, and observe what the Lord your God requires: Walk in God's ways, and keep God's decrees and commands, God's laws and requirements, as written in the Law of Moses, so that you may prosper in all you do and wherever you go, and that the Lord will keep this promise: If your descendants watch how they live, and if they walk faithfully before God with all their heart and soul, you will never fail to have a descendant on the throne of Israel.'[vi]

"The old king was then overcome with exhaustion and lay down to sleep. On that same night, David, the first great king of Israel, my father, was gathered unto his fathers and I ascended to the throne. In the commotion surrounding my father's death and my coronation, I forgot all about the so-called Gift, swallowed up by the kingdom left to me."

Upon hearing this, I felt cautiously elated. I knew this information could in fact lead us to the Gift and the hope Solomon was seeking. However, by the look on the king's face and the tone of his voice, he seemed confused by my interest in the Gift and skeptical of its importance.

So I asked, "May I tell you a little about the Gift in the hands of those who came before you?" The king placidly conceded, attempting a smile at the thought of a silly and meaningless story.

"Why not?" he replied.

Encouraged, I pressed forward with enthusiasm. "Many have conjectured that the Gift was somehow given to man from God in Abraham's day. In this case, it would have been handed down among the patriarchs and remained hidden among Joseph's bones in Egypt. Moses, keeping the ancient promise to include the body of Joseph in the great exodus, also received and used the Gift as he led the children of Israel into the promised inheritance, the land of Canaan. More than likely, Joshua would have entered the Promised Land with the Gift and passed it along. However, the judges often overlooked the Gift until the time of Samuel, the mighty judge and prophet.

"Samuel was charged with anointing the first great king in Israel, a task he cautiously fulfilled, preferring that God alone be recognized as the only true King in Israel. It took Samuel several times to fulfill his charge. Samuel first anointed Saul, a striking man—strong, intelligent, gifted, and clever. Saul was a charmer, a real crowd pleaser, and easy on the eyes. Saul was definitely the people's choice—a heroic, aggressive, leader. However, Saul's style masked his substance. Like a hidden viper ready to strike, it was what Saul kept from view that made him most dangerous to himself and everyone else.

"No matter what Saul did or whom he did it for, Saul was always completely loyal only to himself. His government was oppressive to his own people. His tastes were served by his treasury. His battles reflected his ambition rather than justice. When Saul served God, he served God in his own unique way. He would do just enough to feign obedience to the Almighty, but the benefit was all his own.

"Well, it goes without saying that Saul neglected the Gift. In fact, it could be said that Saul never really understood or even considered the potential and wonder of the Gift he possessed. So he casually and callously disregarded it. And the great Gift was cast off into some forgotten corner of the treasury. God's response to Saul's ongoing malignant arrogance was to withdraw His presence and allow Saul's kingdom to collapse beneath the weight of its own self-serving obesity. While this process took place, Samuel continued his search for a suitable king."

Something at this point in the story caught Solomon's attention. His face softened and he leaned forward. I could feel his growing attention and interest.

I continued, "In Bethlehem, the Lord led Samuel to a man named Jessie—your grandfather—who had twelve sons. Upon entering Jessie's camp, Samuel eyed eleven sons, all who met the surface requirements for Saul's replacement. However, before Samuel could repeat the earlier mistake, the Lord prompted Samuel to inquire about the twelfth son, who was out tending the herds.

"When David—your father—arrived, he defied all expectations, for he was merely a boy. David presented the opposite of Saul. This ruddy-cheeked, handsome lad was just a child relegated to caring for the flocks.

"However, David apparently was the Lord's anointed, and Samuel was the Lord's servant. So the oil did flow and the deed was done, or shall we say done again. From that time until his final breath, David continued to defy expectations and surprised both his people and his enemies.

"For you see, your father, David, learned the lessons of the Gift through both use and neglect. David gave glory to God in victory and repented before God of his sins. He did not elevate the Gift above the Giver. David's use of the Gift made him brilliant as you can testify. However, his neglect of the Gift was equally tragic, as you have experienced."

I paused. Suspicious, Solomon interjected, "So all I need is this gift you are talking about and everything will simply work out?"

"I am not sure it will be that easy," I replied. "It is more than the Gift itself; it is about what the Gift can show you."

"Show me?"

"Yes, the Gift will help you see."

"I can see quite well," insisted the king.

"I am sure you can," I replied, "but there are things you cannot see as well."

"What do you mean? What are you trying to say?"

"Well, O King, please, I beg your pardon, but you have sought my help for troubles that are somehow beyond your current ability to understand. Is this not true?"

"Yes, you are correct on that account. I have called upon you." We both sat in silence for a moment.

"Well," said the king in a tone of defensive doubt, "how am I supposed to see with a gift I do not have?"

"That depends on the answer to my next question. What have you done with the Gift your father presented to you on the night you became king?"

A startled look of astonishment came over the king's face, as if surprised by the possibility of both the challenge and opportunity for hope.

CHAPTER VI

he king, having affirmed the Gift's existence and confessed his lapse in memory, still had no idea where it might be. Servants were dispatched throughout the palace in search of the Gift. Before long, it was found in the treasury where it had been haphazardly discarded.

Before us on a small table lay the ancient Gift. I inquired of Solomon, "What else did your father tell you about the Gift?"

Solomon's countenance became blank. "I believe I have told you all I know. If there is anything else, I am unable to recall."

Wanting to proceed with caution, I thought it prudent to say a little more about the Gift before handling it. I began, "The Gift has had a major influence on our people and our relations with others for as long as we can remember. This Gift is a cherished spiritual heirloom of our people, which is why it has been passed down from the hands of our great fathers and mothers from generation to generation. While the Gift has a powerful range of persuasion on its recipients, the Gift itself possesses no magical power. The unique way in which the Gift works, and its rather humble appearance, can be very misleading. So, while the Gift is a highly sought prize, once possessed it has often been neglected or laid aside because it seems powerless and unnecessary."

We sat for awhile, silently gazing at the worn and faded silk purse on the table. I could feel the anticipation growing in the room, my optimism contending with the king's skepticism.

"Shall we open it?" ventured Solomon.

"Yes, I believe now is the right time to do so," I said.

Solomon opened the bag and revealed its contents. With an expression of childlike wonder, he disclosed the ancient contents: two frames, one containing a crude mirror, the other a small window. His initial youthful fascination quickly turned to adult disappointment.

"It does not look like much" was his verdict. "I was expecting a little more considering my needs and your enthusiasm," the king added, sounding dissatisfied.

"Why is that?" I probed.

"I guess I expected to see something . . . greater," the king confessed.

"Greater?"

"Well, I am not quite sure," replied Solomon, confused and at a loss for words.

"Please bear with my repetition, O King. The Gift's rather humble appearance can be very misleading."

Solomon was now silently taking a closer look at the objects on the table before him. I proceeded, "It is the way of our Lord God to bring greatness out of humility, whether in an instrument like the Gift or in a person like you or me. The Lord seeks to do great and ordinary tasks through weak and needy people, servants who yield their lives to God's will, unique ways, and awesome power. Under these conditions God receives the glory that would otherwise be misplaced on God's servants.

"Solomon, as mere instruments we are helpless; but as we yield our availability to God, we will do both large and small things by the Almighty's empowerment. Through these endeavors, God is honored and we will find blessing and contentment. God is pleased to use our crooked lives to draw a straight line in the world.

"Now, your father, David, would humbly use the Gift, inquiring of the Lord as to what God's will might be. As God affirmed plans with David, they would prevail. However, when David would neglect the Gift, attempting to second-guess the mind of God and act under his own impulse, his efforts were in vain and he would fail miserably. David found the same to be true in his human relationships. Through the Gift, he communicated with others and listened to them, and their plans and projects were fruitful. When David merely assumed he understood others, thus neglecting the Gift, he would endure tremendous difficulty and frustration."

As I set my gaze upon the Gift, I asked Solomon, "What do you see on the table?"

He responded, "I see two frames, one enclosing a window, the other a mirror."

I inquired further, "What is the significance of windows and mirrors?"

Solomon did not need to think long about this question and quickly responded, "They enable us to see ourselves, one another, and our world."

I pressed the young king further with a deeper question, "How could that ancient mirror and window enable you to see all that God has promised you, a wisdom that could turn your life around and change the world forever?"

The king silently gazed at the Gift and back at me several times. He appeared puzzled at how such a lowly gift could possibly evoke such a profound and powerful change.

Breaking the silence, the king said, "I do not understand it. I am desperate for something . . . but I just cannot see it."

"Let us hold these thoughts in silence," I suggested, "and consider them for a few days. Then we can return to our conversation." The king reluctantly agreed.

Within a day or two, the young king was up with the sun, eager to continue our conversation about the Gift. Solomon had a few questions but mostly listened as I explained all I could about the Gift. "So, Master, what has been on your heart since we last sat together?"

"I am unable to comprehend how there can be power in such a Gift. It still looks like nothing to me."

"The power of the Gift," I responded, "lies in its ordinary exterior that veils its highly prized insight and wisdom. Most sought-after treasures and objects of power are deceivingly pleasing to the eye, naturally attractive, and desirous. However, like fool's gold, they prove disappointing because their appearance promises more than their worth. The opposite effect is invoked by the Gift. It appears to promise little on account of its humble demeanor, inviting its recipient to take a closer look. Real gold, unlike fool's gold, is rarely lying about on the surface. One must search for it, which often requires some deep digging.

"The ancient window and mirror are instruments that give the power to see with wisdom, but not like we might suspect. These are not divining tools producing information and images through sorcery. Rather, these instruments are symbols that help you to see the importance and power of your relationships. The Gift will guide you in all your relationships so that you can relate to God, others, and yourself with life-changing wisdom. The Gift is designed to bear its maximum influence over you, its possessor, rather than your circumstances or others. The Gift's influence is not merely limited to your major discernments in life. This Gift aims to affect even your basic habitual judgments that are surprisingly important to daily living. Serving as a critically placed marker in the wilderness, the Gift will guide you, keeping your journey on course, lest you become lost and perish."

"But why a window and mirror? I cannot grasp what they mean or how they work," inquired the king.

Again, I could sense the king's growing frustration. "Obviously the Gift includes two instruments: a window and a mirror. One is not more important than the other, nor is there a priority or formula in the way they are used. Each complements the other; both are necessary and must be used in balance and harmony. They each serve as one half of a single gift."

Looking at the king I said, "Let us explore the Gift." Picking up the small window, I examined the ancient wooden frame, smooth by centuries of handling. Within the frame, a small pane of glass offered a transparent view.

I continued, "This window, O King, is your reminder of the great world that lies beyond you. You see outside through this window. Even though you have great power, wealth, and authority, much more comprises this world than simply you. You will always be best served to realize that while you may assert influential might in the world, the world does not revolve around you." I handed Solomon the window.

"Through this Gift, you have a window to the world. You have the ability to observe how God is moving within creation. The window invites you to consider, 'Lord, how might I serve You and do Your will in this day and place?' In doing so, you will receive direction and inspiration for all of your decisions, demands, and challenges. Like the notch on a bow that gives your eye focus to shoot the arrow, so the window draws your eye's focus towards God.

"Through this window you will no doubt see others. Many of these will be worthy partners in your divine endeavors. Some will need your patience, guidance, wisdom, and encouragement in order that they too might discover their place in the plans of the Almighty. Still others will prove to be your enemies, which you will learn to treat with justice, compassion, and even love."

"So, the window is my reminder of the world of others around me as well as God before me?" the king offered, warming up to the possibility of the Gift.

"Yes!" I encouraged. "This window will give you a clear view of what you are doing, where you are going, and who you are with. It will enable you to see the importance of the relationships you share with God and others. In this way God intends to impart the wisdom that will deliver you from the deception of your own narrow understanding. Your own wisdom and self-importance creates skepticism of God and suspicion of others, tempting you to go your own way in your own strength. This way is the road to arrogance, which leads away from God and others towards isolation.

"Dear King, just as you post a watchman on the city walls to serve the interests and safety of your kingdom, the Gift of your window serves to remind you of the presence of God and the blessings of others. From the view through your window you will grow in an ever-expanding fellowship and community with all you behold—even your enemies. You will give God the glory and praise for all you see. In fact, God will unveil plans for you through all the people you see and come to know. Your life will be full and complete as you work through the difficult but desirous demands of loving God and others.

"This view from your window reveals an arduous but fruitful challenge of living in peace with God and others. However, your view also spares you from a dreadful life of embittered loneliness." I noticed the king nodding in approval as my words were being received in his heart.

Next, I picked up the mirror, a sheet of highly polished metal that oddly reflected the image of its viewer. It too was encompassed by an old wooden frame. I could still make out some detail carved around it.

I proceeded, "The mirror is the reminder of yourself and who you really are. While taking hold of the mirror, you will behold more than your physical face. You will hold in your hand a means of examination and personal discernment." I handed Solomon the mirror, and he gazed into it as if searching for his very soul. I wondered what Solomon could see and what it felt like for him.

"The mirror enables you to face yourself—all you are doing, how you are feeling, and what your motives are. Beholding the mirror intently will reflect both the positive and virtuous, as well as the negative and dishonorable characteristics of your life. A healthy examination should be neither a morbid review of all your failings, nor a whitewashed recounting of your successes. Your true reflection in this mirror should divulge and balance both the nobility and need of your life, thus revealing a solid foundation for building healthy love for yourself."

I noticed that the king was still intently looking at his own reflection so I asked him, "What is it like to see your reflection?"

"I am not sure," replied the king. "This is all very new, but I desire to know more. Please continue."

"As you faithfully gaze at your reflection, more will be revealed. You will begin to see and accept your whole life, all of you—good and bad. You will find the strength to take responsibility and be accountable for what is not going well in your life. It is not easy to weigh and measure your life honestly. You need help facing difficulty. This is why the mirror is a Gift.

"Furthermore, you will learn to graciously accept commendations as your life warrants. This too can be awkward. Accepting praise and thanks can be overwhelming, making one feel undeserving, even embarrassed. Seeing your real reflection in the mirror will cause you to face and balance your life's shortcomings and virtues, which leads you to maturity, knowing who you really are."

"Are you saying the mirror beckons me to look deeper within my life beneath the image of my face?"

"Yes! That is correct."

The king then recalled a story. "I remember hunting with my father in the forest. We came upon a small, still pond. It was the first time I had seen myself completely reflected. I was fascinated with what I saw; I had never considered what I might look like. It was strange to see myself for the first time. I remember thinking, *Is that who I am? Is that what I really look like?*" The king turned his focus toward me. "What might this mirror show me?" he asked.

"In the mirror God intends to impart wisdom that can deliver you from the pitfalls of vanity and conceit, resulting in pride. Swelling pride demands mounting a tireless defense of constant explanation. You become consumed in unending attempts to build and fortify your appearance while vindicating your behavior. Your misjudgment seeks justification in blaming others while making excuses for yourself.

"Failure to reach your prideful ambitions leads to self-contempt. Equally destructive as pride, contempt reaches an opposite outcome by turning your fault-finding inward; you begin blaming yourself for everything. Your life becomes savagely dismantled, rendering you the victim of your own pity. However, with your mirror you begin to honestly see who you are and humbly receive yourself. You learn to embrace what you do, both good and bad. The corrosive pride and inward blaming of contempt will give way to humility. Though humility is not easy, it remains a powerful advocate for discovering who we are and desire to be. Humility blesses us with a sober and frank discernment of our lives, saving us from the deceptive forces of pride and contempt."

As our discussion continued, the low burning lamps became an indication of how long we had been talking and our need to rest. I had much more to share with the king, but we concluded our conversation, taking time for silence, to allow our thoughts to sink in.

Chapter VII

 expected to see the king the following day, but I did not. I assumed he stayed to himself, pondering the Gift and its meaning. Within a few days, I was summoned into his presence. Solomon greeted me warmly and confirmed my assumption that he had spent time meditating on the Gift. He confided and embraced his own lingering suspicions with three very practical questions.

Solomon began, "I am grateful to God for His mysterious Gift. However, I am still unclear of its purpose and why the Lord has given it to me."

I addressed the king, "Your questions are most important. On the high place at Mt. Gibeon, the Lord made a promise to you—true?"

"Yes."

"And what was that promise?"

"That I would be wise, having the wisdom of a discerning heart."

"So, how is that going to happen?"

"I do not know; that is why I am turning to you for help on these matters."

"Well, in order for you to receive this promise and be wise your entire life, you must be a lifelong seeker of God, who imparts wisdom to you. The Gift is the means God is using to remind you of your original desire—God and wisdom. The Gift is also a reminder that God and God alone is the source of the wisdom you seek and need. As you learn to see with the window and mirror, you will be in constant view of the opportunities and difficulties ahead of you on life's journey. Using the Gift, you will turn to God, the Lord's promise will be fulfilled, and you will have sufficient wisdom for all occasions.

Solomon interrupted, "But what is God asking of me? What is it that I must do to inherit such a Gift and receive such a promise?"

"Master, now we have come to the very heart of the issue, have we not? God's chief desire for you and all humanity is to grow beyond the shallow self where most people exist and engage our deeper selves in him. This way of the deep self is indeed holy, mysterious, and formidable. However, it is this path that leads to a life of wisdom, your original desire and request of God. The window and mirror are instruments designed and used by God to deliver you from your shallow self, releasing you to your deeper self.

"The aim of the window is to free you from the arrogance of self-importance with its debilitating isolation and fruitlessness. God's wisdom seeks to free you for community and fellowship with Himself and others, in caring love and unity. Likewise, the mirror's purpose is to free you from the pride of self-righteousness with its constant excuses and paralyzing self-defense, so that you might be free to be humble, content, and at peace with yourself and thereby at peace with God and others.

"Dear King, as you ponder the Gift, desiring to understand it in the freedom and safety of this conversation, it is indeed very natural to ask, 'What am I to do?' However, our compassionate God in heaven realizes that our earthly and human condition can do very little. Our lives resemble those lost at sea, shipwrecked and adrift in the storm. In reality, all of us are desperate and drowning. Our life-threatening circumstances do not usually afford us the luxury of questions. We are all spiritually lost at sea, too busy thrashing about, desperately grabbing at whatever might come along and save us.

"O King, this Gift has come along. It is yours for the taking. You have asked for wisdom, and the Lord God Almighty has promised and provided. The Gift is already in your hands. You cannot do anything; you cannot merit or earn this. The Gift is a gift.

"God's design for you is to grab hold of the Gift. In doing so, your shallow self will be overwhelmed and shrink. As you embrace your deep self, it will expand. This is the ancient wisdom that leads you to God and makes you wise. This will lead you in the way of humility, at peace with yourself and in fellowship with God and others. Furthermore, when the king is influenced by the Gift toward true regard for God, others, and self, will not the subjects of the land benefit as they take notice and follow your example?"

After a thoughtful silence, Solomon asked his third question, "As I use the Gift, what pitfalls are hidden along the way that might draw me off course? What temptations lie ahead for me along this way?"

"O King, I must caution you in regards to four temptations. These are dire warnings to which you must adhere. Every privilege contains a responsibility, and even with the Gift comes stewardship, a care you must address. Therefore, take note and listen; be on your guard concerning the temptations you will face."

1. Be forewarned of the temptation to withhold the Gift.

"While the Gift you possess is personal, it is not private. Most certainly the Gift you hold is yours, but within your grasp is the possibility of either blessing or evil for our entire kingdom. The Gift enables you to see both within and outside of yourself. In doing so, the Gift will direct your course in relationship to God and others. It will be tempting to assume that your use of the Gift narrowly pertains to you and your concerns. Nothing could be further from the truth. Your handling of the Gift will affect all who affirm your initiatives and work with you. Those who oppose you and work against you will receive consequences for their actions.

"Your stewardship of the Gift will touch everyone just like the ripples on a small pond that go out in all directions when it is disturbed by a single stone. Either your shallow or deep self will directly or indirectly influence the outcome of many. Your Gift is communal, not individual."

2. Be forewarned of the temptation to master the Gift.

"This Gift is not a source in itself, and it carries no magical power. In this way it can guarantee nothing. No exact steps or formulas are used with the Gift. The Gift is not about the Gift, but rather what the Gift points towards—God, others, and yourself. The Gift's purpose is not its own realization or attention. Rather, the Gift creates visionary light that enables you to clearly see your relationships.

"You may be tempted to think you can maneuver the Gift, when in reality the Gift is molding and changing you. Therefore, the Gift is highly interactive and social, rather than a goal-oriented tool in your hands. The Gift uniquely influences you, the recipient, to embrace your deep self, out of which will flow right relationships. Your Gift is relational, not mechanical."

3. Be forewarned of the temptation to reverse the Gift.

"While the Gift does not respond to a set formula, the Gift must be used according to its intention. As we have discussed, the window gives you a view of your outside world in relation to yourself. The mirror, on the other hand, gives you a view of yourself in relation to the outside world. This being so, you must be careful to use the window to see God and others, intending to mature in those relationships. Likewise, carefully use the mirror to check yourself, examining who and what you really are in relationship to God and others. In this way your shallow self decreases while your deep self increases.

"Beware in times of difficulty, when things do not go well, when failure visits. Also, beware in times when all seems well, when success abounds. At these times, a subtle but dangerous temptation threatens you to misuse the Gift by inverting and abusing it. In bad times you may find yourself looking out the window in order to blame someone for your bad fortune and excuse yourself. Resist, use your mirror, and look within to find the root of your problem.

"In good days, you may preen before the mirror seeking admiration and commendation. Resist, use your window, look outward giving thanks to God and affirming others for the season of goodness. These reversed uses of the Gift strengthen the shallow self and weaken your deep self. Your Gift is vulnerable to misuse, not immune to it."

4. Be forewarned of the temptation to neglect the Gift.

"Finally, the Gift is rendered completely powerless through neglect. This may be the most perilous temptation of all. Possession of the Gift is meaningless unless it is used. You may think that possession of the Gift is enough, and you will use it if you need it. To have true wisdom, though, you must use the Gift all the time. Possession alone only creates false security if the Gift is not engaged.

"Understand, the Gift is neither a talisman nor a charm. It will come about in a time of great confidence, wonderful progress, and success that this cunning temptation appears. You will say to yourself, *I do not believe I need the Gift any longer. I am quite sure I can handle this on my own for now.* Herein lies the paradox of this snare. Just when circumstances seem so wonderful, when the purpose of the Gift appears complete, this is the exact time when the Gift is most necessary.

"O King, you must know that each of your forbearers who possessed this divine Gift fell into the darkness of this temptation. Just as the light of the Gift shone its brightest, it was extinguished by the hand that needed it most. My lord, I implore you, take heed of this crafty and most dangerous tendency. Your Gift is nullified by neglect."

At these sobering words, Solomon sat in silence weighing these temptations in his heart. With a wave of his hand, Solomon concluded the conversation and silently excused me, his servant Zadok, from his chambers.

Chapter VIII

inter had now arrived in Jerusalem, which can be surprisingly cold, a possibility we inhabitants never seem prepared for. I had not seen the king in weeks. He had not called on the service of his priest. I suspected he was experimenting with the Gift. This morning, thick clouds covered the city and deposited a thin layer of snow over Zion. The weather cast a nasty mood over the city, which matched the king's attitude when he summoned me that day.

I could see frustration and anger in the king's eyes even before he spoke. Solomon began, "What is this so-called Gift? It is no blessing, just an evil curse—a curse that is driving me mad."

I responded, "What is it about the Gift that finds you so troubled, my lord?"

"It does not work," he responded. "I cannot get the Gift to work for me. It seems to be working against me."

"How so?" I inquired.

"The window and the mirror vex me with such a wide range of emotions, thoughts, and responses. Every time I look, I become upset at all I see. This cannot be good, can it?"

"Say more, my king, please."

"When I look out the window, all I see are the problems of the kingdom. I see all that is not right, things that must be built or mended. I become overwhelmed and discouraged. I know not where to begin. It is all far too much for me. Most of the people I see through the window seem to be either incompetent or untrustworthy. I doubt their abilities and see their efforts as insufficient for the task. I feel like blaming them for all my troubles. I realize my judgments are harsh, neither fair nor helpful; yet, this is how I feel.

"When I look in the mirror, I am confused, seeing a person that does not appeal to me. The man I see is irritated and irrational. In the mirror, I condemn myself, then I defend myself. I attempt to justify myself by finding fault with my life's circumstances. I compare myself to others and judge them in the hopes of making myself look or feel better. Yet, there is no true vindication in all of this.

"I end up returning to self-condemnation, loathing, and hatred. Drowning in pity, I blame myself for everything and why not? I'm desperate to fix the muddle that has become my life. I feel that I am thrashing around for a way out. Deep beneath these layers of failure, I am seeking the approval and acceptance of others. Even as the king who appears to know it all and have it all, I am a mess of needs, mistakes, desires, and broken dreams. What am I doing wrong?"

I paused for a moment in silence to provide a space for the king's honest revelations. I considered all I had heard and collected my thoughts.

Then I began, "Dear King, it is certainly not that you are using the Gift incorrectly. Rather, you have entered into the process of the Gift. In that process it will take time for you to understand its benefits. The Gift must reveal to you its brutal truth before you will be able to receive its hopeful promise.

"First, you receive a startling raw glimpse of who you really are and what you have become. In this stage of the process, the Gift reveals a rather ugly self-portrait that is very difficult to look at, much less embrace."

"Yes! This Gift feels more like a weapon," the king interjected.

"How does that feel?" I asked.

"It feels like I am being wounded and hurt by the Gift," Solomon responded freely. "I want to protect and defend myself from its painful accusations. I doubt the wisdom of the Gift, second-guessing God while my self-confidence erodes to nothing. Yet a small voice still urges me forward, but I do not know how."

"What is that voice saying?" I asked.

"I think it is urging me to stay with the Gift and trust in God," the king responded thoughtfully.

"Listen to that voice," I encouraged. "Move forward with the understanding that you are honestly reacting to your own image and your view of others. While this part of the process is very uncomfortable, it is necessary that you suffer through it, realizing the utter darkness of your shallow self. This painful knowledge signals both the need and motivation that lead to change.

"Next will come a helpful vision, a new future in which you begin to see the promises of the life that lies just before you. In this stage, the Gift reveals the hope of your life with others from God's point of view. You will not comprehend this view in the Gift until you accept your profound need of this new vision. God will invite you to see more than just your shallow self by revealing a glimpse of your deep self as well. God is prepared to give you a vision of yourself and others that promises more encouragement, hope, and peace in this difficult life than you have ever considered possible.

"Soon, when you look through the mirror, you will begin to see yourself created in God's image. The face you behold in the mirror will also contain the image of the Almighty. Through the window, you will begin to see others who also bear God's image, like you—the ever emerging deep self becoming exposed. A shadowy likeness of the distressing shallow self will always linger. However, like our eyes becoming accustomed to light as we leave the darkness, our spiritual eyes will find their focus on God that will change our view of self and others forever."

"What am I to do next?" the king inquired.

"It may be less about doing and more about yielding," I responded. "Consider this. One, you cannot control the Gift and it does not control you. It is merely a guide that can enable you to be wise, having an eye for God's vision and a heart to fulfill it. Two, you will only be able to see a little at a time. This is a process in a relationship with God—no one gets it all at once. Three, the Gift brings you to God first and foremost. In God comes the new vision of yourself and others. Therefore, you must release your effort in self-mending. Realize your need for God, and let God bring the change to your life. As you are touched by God's truth, let go of the tempting, false ideas of your old self. As you release your shallow self, your deep self begins to emerge and grow. Become willing to change, yet not willful in pursuing change."

In an encouraged tone the king asked, "Where do I go from here?"

It seemed providential that he used the word "go" in his question. For in the course of our conversation, we agreed that he should go—get away, retreat, and refocus on God. King David had spent much time in the desert and wrote, "Be still and know that I am God."[vii] Moses and the fathers and mothers before him all found their way with God through the desert.

An elaborate scheme was developed among Solomon's leaders in which the king could leave without his people or his enemies knowing he was not occupying the throne in Jerusalem. Solomon was encouraged by the idea of being away, taking time to think about his life, to consider the ways of God and the strange Gift he had received. On his way south, he could visit his father's retreat at Engedi. In disguise, he would inspect his great mines in Timna, his ports in Eilat, and the exotic markets of Petra. At least for a while he might be free of the burden of his reign and kingly role.

DEBRE DAMO

Present Day

CHAPTER IX

s the Abba begins reading the next chapter, he is interrupted by a loud call from the bell tower outside. It reminds me of Islam's call to prayer. At that very moment, monks began to gather in the sanctuary quietly, seating themselves, as if students attentively waiting for class to begin.

The Abba says nothing. Concerned by the gathering, I look at him and he asks, "Is there a problem?"

I hesitate, not wanting to offend. The old monk encourages me to speak, beckoning with soft, clear eyes that unlock my tongue. "The loud noise outside sounds like the Islamic call to prayer. Why is everyone gathering?"

The Abba smiles, then says, "In the early days of the prophet Mohammed, he and his family received much persecution. The Ethiopian Church offered the prophet's family hospitality and refuge in the holy city of Axum. We have called our community to prayer in this way for hundreds of years prior to Islam taking up the tradition. Our monks gather for prayer at midday, seeking God's provision and strength to overcome the tempter of laziness, the 'noonday devil.' After prayer, we retire for our main meal of the day."

Their service is simple but rich, like a tasty appetizer or rare delicacy, very small, yet surprisingly satisfying. They begin with a chant, the Scripture is read, an interpretation given, and they pray in silence. I follow the crowd to the meal that is held in a humble, open-air refectory with some covering for shade. We sit on the dirt floor in small groups around low tables. We are served *injera*, a cultural meal and culinary staple of Ethiopia.

At first glance, the injera's appearance resembles a typical extra large pizza. However, from that point the similarities end. The "crust" is made from the *tef* grain that offers carbohydrates to the diet but little nutritional value. The tef is prepared by soaking it in water until fermented (about three days), then cooking it like a huge pancake on a griddle over an open fire. The finished product has a foam rubber texture, and to my palate tastes rather sour. The toppings include *wat* (two kinds of stew): *kai wat* (red) spicy hot, and *alicha wat* (yellowish) very bland. Boiled meats of mysterious origins called *tibbs* are often included. A variety of vegetables are also added. The finishing touch is a hardboiled egg or two.

The meal is eaten communally around the table, everyone using their right hand. This is tricky for me, being left-handed. However, I learn quickly after receiving groans of rebuke upon reaching in with my left hand. During the course of the meal, the boiled egg is offered to a guest, if present. I figured this out as I noticed the egg slowly but intentionally being nudged in my direction.

As the egg comes toward me, bobbing in a swamp of wat and tibbs, it is being blessed by every hand on the table before it reaches its final destination. When the egg is within range of my right hand, I realize the duty that lies before me. I know if I put too much thought into the task, I will end up a rude and unappreciative guest. So I pick up the egg, throw caution to the wind, and quickly eat it.

I am in the middle of their unique world, so different from my own. By my observation, the fellowship among these monks is genuine and joy filled. They live and pray in humble gratefulness before God, separated from the entire world below them. They not only allow my presence, but they also welcome and honor me as their special guest with no recognizable hesitation.

Looking around, I catch myself immersed and delighted in the enthusiasm of this moment. The monks' cheerfulness and acceptance is infectious. They embody the glad and sincere sounds of temple bells, calling forth a small but deep stream of happiness from somewhere inside me. Its current is full of peace and healing, so I give myself to its flow. I feel a tremendous sense of divine and human love.

It occurs to me again that this experience may be the beginning of something more, a kind of divine appointment. I recalled the guardian of the Ark in Axum telling me about this place. Had he invited me or sent me? Regardless, here I am in a 1,400 year old monastery, listening to an ancient story—the Book of Zadok. What am I to make of this? Where did they get this book? I feel like pinching myself thinking, *Is this all merely chance?* For the moment, the answers elude me. So in the midst of this awesome experience I give myself to prayer for strength to overcome skepticism, perhaps my own noonday devil.

"Dear Lord Jesus, You know my heart, lead me by the power of Your presence that I might remain open and receptive to simply follow You this day. Amen."

After lunch the Abba takes me for a walk to the far side of the plateau.

"We come now to a very holy place," says the Abba as we make a short descent off the backside of the mountain. The trail leads to a shelf twenty yards or so below the mountaintop. "This is where our hermits come to live, pray, and die. No one is present in the hermitage at this time. I thought it might be of interest to you."

From the shelf, a beautiful view of the valley is below. Against the cliff side are three, maybe four small holes about two feet in diameter. Each is covered with round, hewn stones; they appear as oversized portholes along the side of a boat.

The Abba rolls away a stone to reveal the hermit's cave. The cave itself is about ten feet wide by twenty feet deep and only four feet high. On one side I can see where one or perhaps two hermits might sleep, rest, and pray in alcoves along the wall. On the opposite side are stacked bones and skulls of the fathers and brothers whose lives and prayers on this earth were spent, their spirits and souls now departed, leaving only their dusty shells as a memorial to their devotion and intercession. The Abba gestures with his hand, an invitation to crawl in. I consider it but respectfully decline. I do not want to mock this hallowed ground with tasteless curiosity, or is this simply my polite refusal of the Abba's invitation to die to myself in prayer? I'm not sure which it is. We walk back in silence.

Coming to the edge of the compound, the Abba diverts our steps to a small rise overlooking the rest of the plateau, as well as a 360-degree view of the valley below. The hill is covered with an umbrella shaped acacia tree. Under the shade of that tree, an elaborate tradition is being prepared for us—coffee ceremony or *buna*. In our presence, the coffee beans are roasted in a frying pan over a charcoal fire. The roasted beans are ground in a crude, wooden mortar. The coffee grounds are then boiled in a large kettle. The space around the fire where we sit is covered with freshly cut greens, and incense is thrown into the fire for an aromatic effect. Along with our coffee we are offered fresh popped corn that is seasoned with sugar. All this is a delight to our senses—interesting to watch, wonderful to smell, and delicious to eat and drink.

As we relax, enjoying buna and our view of the whole world below, I decide to initiate a discussion. "Abba, may I ask a few questions?"

"It is possible," he replies.

"Why are you here?"

"What are you asking, my friend?"

"I guess I want to know what you are doing here and why. Of course it must be a real blessing to be up here far from all the worldly cares."

"What do you mean by 'blessing'?" replies the Abba.

"Well, it's very quiet here, right? Life is slow and simple; and you have all this time to yourself. It seems kind of ideal, even inviting, yet I'm not sure what to think. I guess that's why I'm asking you."

In a firm but kind voice the Abba responds, "We are not here for ourselves; we are here for you."

This wasn't the answer I expected, I thought to myself, *What do you mean, you are here for me?* I catch myself reacting.

"That's right," the Abba replies calmly. "You are correct about life here in the monastery. It is quiet, slow, and simple; therefore, we have time to be here for you. May I ask you a question, Pastor Jeff?"

"Sure," I respond, still wondering about his strange answer.

"How would you describe the pace of your life back home in your village and church?"

"Well, I'd have to say it's busy, too busy actually. That's why I'm here on sabbatical."

"True," the Abba affirms. "One more question please."

"Certainly."

"Pastor Jeff, as the shepherd of your flock, how much time do you spend in prayer over your sheep in comparison to everything else you do in your priesthood?"

I sense a hesitancy to answer, not because I don't know, but because I can't bring myself to say it. As the silence grows, so does my conviction. "Very little in comparison to all else." I notice I'm speaking in a whisper, looking far away down in the valley, wishing I were there . . .

Very gently the Abba begins, "That is why we are here; we are praying for you. We—"

I interrupt, "How do you pray for us? How do you know our requests?"

The Abba responds, holding his ground yet speaking in love, "And you claim to know everyone and their needs in your busyness?" He continues calmly with utmost respect, "Most people over the face of the earth do not really know what they want, much less what they need. That is why we pray for you, the church. As I was saying, we are called by Jesus to pray from this holy mountain. We are not here retreating from the world, we are here serving Christ and the world."

As the Abba spoke tenderly to me, I could feel my defenses recede and my body relax again. I could hear his voice continue.

"We do not know everyone or their needs but God does, so we seek the divine heart of Jesus and intercede for our broken world. We pray that people everywhere would come to know themselves, share their lives with their neighbors, and love God with all their hearts. We believe this prayer is spreading the hope of Jesus and His kingdom to every nation around the world.

"Jeff, we are blessed to be here and fulfill God's call. Yet, we are mere mortals, we are often lonely, and we become fearful and even selfish. Therefore, we take time to pray for ourselves as well." As quiet descended upon us, peace enveloped us.

As my mood begins to mellow, I reflect on the three hundred men in this mountaintop monastery praying for the world. Being prayed and cared for in this way had never occurred to me. Their intercession is sustaining me! I could sense a subtle shift in the loneliness that often shadows me. I take hope and comfort in receiving their prayers for me. It is a small but profound breakthrough. I can feel a burden being lifted. It is wonderful to be still and notice for a moment the amazing gift of God's love and provision. God's care over all things is abundant and complete. In times like these, I wonder why I ever become anxious or lonely. My mind is as far from worry as I am from home.

Finally the Abba broke our silence saying, "It is time to return to our story."

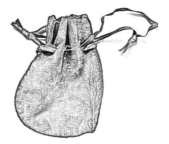

The

Book of Zadok

Part 2

Jerusalem 970 BC

✠

CHAPTER X

The Abba returned to his reading from the Book of Zadok...

 olomon's stealth sabbatical had a wonderful effect on Zion. In his absence his commanders and builders restarted the projects that King David had begun. They acquired and prepared the materials for the temple and palace of the new king. The busyness and industry lifted the people's spirits and was good for the economy. The plan succeeded in two ways. It concealed the king's whereabouts, while invigorating life in the kingdom.

The king's adventure was also life changing. Solomon had lived a reasonably sheltered life; being out on the edges of the realm gave him exposure to life in the wider world. While traveling, the king experienced many different people, places, cultures, and ideas—most in contrast to life as he had always known it. He now realized the vast wealth of his kingdom and the reach of his royal hand. In the slower pace and rest of his journey, he gained perspective and insight on his otherwise busy life. Solomon took time to consider how to manage the affairs of the kingdom. He reflected on how he would choose his priorities and where he might concentrate his efforts. He was also coming to terms with himself: Whom had he become? Whom was he going to be and why?

Solomon appeared more at home with himself and his role as king. He seemed content with himself for the first time in his young life. He had a keen sense of God's presence, provision, and power. He was finding a way he had never experienced apart from the Gift— a personal, affirming encounter with God. Solomon was getting to know the God he had met on Mt. Gibeon.

He spent more time alone with God, meditating and contemplating the deeper issues of life and its application to his daily realities. Solomon was beginning to welcome rather than resist this life changing process the Gift had encouraged. He was never far from the Gift, using the small window and mirror often as his vantage point, his measuring rod, to give him wisdom in all things large and small.

The king was less anxious and reluctant concerning his role and responsibilities. He began to employ the services and abilities of others, allowing them to do their work in his behalf and the kingdom.

His ability to accept and relate to others took an amazing leap. His guarded suspicion of others was giving way to engaging interest. The possibility of new partnerships and relationships with others emerged. When he returned I saw on his face joy and excitement. He appeared hungry for relationships. With all their blessings and problems, Solomon was being drawn into the wonder, mystery, and messiness of life.

Upon his return, we began to meet regularly. During our conversations, Solomon would share his life and all he was learning. I, in turn, would listen to his life, his thoughts, and his feelings. I would express to the king what I was hearing. I might ask him questions that would enable him to clarify the story of his own heart. I would listen as well to the voice of God in my own heart so that we might both incline our ears to God's spiritual voice and movement in our lives.

As an outcome of Solomon's time alone with God, he began to bring to our conversations his writings and notes. As it was written of the great lawgiver, "Moses recorded the stages in their journey."[viii] So Solomon recorded his spiritual journey. As he fell deeper in love with God, his writing reflected the imparted wisdom of a father to a son. Many would later misunderstand this, assuming that Solomon was writing to his own earthly son, but this was not necessarily the case. Foremost in Solomon's mind was God's wisdom (as a Father) addressed to himself (a son) as God had promised on Mt. Gibeon.

Solomon wrote as follows:

My son, if you accept my words and store up my commands within you, turning your ear to wisdom and applying your heart to understanding, and if you call out for insight and cry aloud for understanding, and if you look for it as for silver and search for it as for hidden treasure, then you will understand the fear of the Lord and find the knowledge of God. For the Lord gives wisdom, and from his mouth come knowledge and understanding.[ix]

There was also a very unique, if not peculiar, voice to the wisdom that Solomon was writing. For wisdom's voice would often appear feminine as a woman—"she." You see, Solomon was not only in love with God, the Giver of wisdom, he was also in love with wisdom herself. The Gift turned Solomon's focus to God while God, in turn, revealed the wisdom that had been promised. The fulfillment of that promise led Solomon from a life buried in fear, responsibility, and dread to a life of joy, learning, and trusting in God's wisdom.

Solomon, elated by this new life, wrote of his attraction to wisdom in romantic imagery. He was pursuing wisdom as he would court a beautiful woman, a helpmate, companion, best friend, or lover. For Solomon, true wisdom enabled him to lovingly attend to God, others, and himself. The king envisioned these three loves as a strong cord of three strands. Seeking wisdom and living it was life's primary pursuit. Solomon wrote:

Wisdom is supreme; therefore get wisdom. Though it cost all you have, get understanding. Esteem her, and she will exalt you; embrace her, and she will honor you. She will set a garland of grace on your head and present you with a crown of splendor.[x]

Wisdom reposes in the heart of the discerning and even among fools she lets herself be known.[xi]

Early in the king's writing, he penned what he regarded as the core of all wisdom, the power source of all life, the vantage point at which both the mirror and the window were always directing his gaze.

Trust in the Lord with all your heart and lean not on your own understanding; in all your ways acknowledge God, and he will make your paths straight.[xii]

For Solomon this brief passage summarized the essence of God's wisdom as revealed to him in the Gift. True wisdom is issued through a trusting relationship with the Lord God of heaven; it is deposited in the hearts, not the minds, of seekers; it exceeds all common sense and human understanding; it must be applied to all situations, large and small; it will lead one in the best path possible, whether we realize it at the time or not.

The king was particularly pleased because he believed these few but powerful revelations were an inspired response to his earthly father's heart cry.

Search me, O God, and know my heart; test me and know my anxious thoughts. See if there is any offensive way in me, and lead me in the way everlasting.[xiii]

Chapter XI

n one occasion when I was summoned into the king's presence, I found his countenance was subdued. I noticed a mood shift but concealed my concern. I decided that listening might be better than confrontation, in hopes that he might feel free to disclose his own condition. The king was eager to begin our conversation.

"I fear I am beginning to understand the veil of Moses," the king declared.

"How so?" I responded tentatively.

"Well, when Moses returned from the presence of the Lord, the Torah explains that his face was veiled, for the glory of the Lord was too great and overwhelmed the people."

"Yes?"

"In time the glory would fade. Sometimes Moses would remain veiled so that others would not perceive the diminished presence on Moses' face. Moses not only veiled the presence of the Lord, he hid its absence as well." Solomon paused then continued, "Zadok, was Moses fearful of his own weakness and what others might conclude from it?"

"It is a real possibility," I conceded. "Why do you ask?"

"I believe I too fear my weakness. In fact, I know I do; I always have. I have enjoyed the presence of the Lord, felt His power, goodness, and strength; but I still have doubts. Sometimes I am not sure where God is. He seems distant to me and I long for His return. During my journey I saw the presence of God everywhere and through everyone, using the window. It was powerful. I believed then that anything was possible. I saw myself in the mirror as well. I faced a lifetime of fear. I came to see and believe that God desired to use me. So I came home with my discoveries, a ball of fire ready to burn for God, to be a bright and mighty light for God's glory. I wanted to be like the sun rising over Mt. Nebo by day, and the moon and stars forming the earth's canopy by night."

"Yes, I recall your enthusiasm!" I encouraged.

"My fire seems to have diminished, like low burning embers late in the night. My bold light feels like the last flickers of a lamp whose oil is spent, whose wick is all but consumed. Now that I am home, the things of this world and the trappings of life are increasingly distracting. My time with God has been disrupted, vandalized by the urgencies of my days. I have removed my eyes from God, and my mirror and window often remain in their purse.

"I need the Gift's help, but I foolishly refuse to take the time to reach for it. I feel the daunting weight of my calling and task, indeed too big for one such as me. How have I fallen away so quickly and so hard? I long to have a veil like Moses to hide behind. I simply want to hide my weakness on days like these and just plow through. I know this too is folly, but this is how I feel." The king paused in thought.

"What if you veil your fear and weakness?" I inquired.

"If I hide such things, they will not flee. Fear and weakness will make a home in me if I protect and hide them in my heart. Yet, my feelings of helplessness are real as well. I do not want them, yet I hang on to them; these paralyzing thoughts are relentless. Like a roof that gives way under too much rain, I feel as though I am crumbling. When the storms of doubt and fear seem so strong, moving on is difficult."

"What is driving this storm within you?" I asked.

The king sat in silence for a while. When he began, he spoke in a vague, dreamy voice as one thinking out loud.

"I suppose the voice from the storm could be the words of my shallow self," he said hesitating as he continued. "I cling to these words, old descriptions of myself because I have heard them all my life. These familiar voices have become comfortable, I know them.

The wisdom from these voices seems to have helped me in the past, or have they? In some odd way these words seem real to me even if they are untrue; they explain and excuse me.

"The words tempt me to veil my shallow self in an attempt to keep it hidden. I can so clearly hear the voice in my ear say, 'You know how to live your old way, when your new way is too much work, too difficult for you just now. You can still lean on your own understanding, as you need, from time to time.' I find strange consolation in the voice of the storm. Why can I not continue in my familiar ways?"

The king stopped as if he had answered his own questions. He began to tear up. With words broken by emotion, he admitted to himself out loud, "It amazes me how willing I am to settle for the false security and empty power of my shallow self. My old ways are deceivingly comforting and tempting. But I want real life; I desire to live, and not merely pretend to live. I long to be complete, whole, true, and real. I seek the eye-opening Gift that reveals God's view, setting me free to experience life with all its pain and joy. I must plug my ears to the lies of the storm attempting to make me feel better with broken promises and deadly excuses. It is essential that I listen and pay attention to how I feel, while at the same time not be ruled or overwhelmed by my emotions. My feelings are tools to knowing myself, but they are a poor compass in seeking life's direction."

"And when you plug your ears to the storm, what comes next?"

"I am not sure," the king replied. "I guess I work with the Gift and keep learning to hear the voice of God. Hopefully I can be patient with myself, trust God, and respect others as I learn to live my life."

Solomon was quiet and still as he came to peace with his words. The king looked exhausted by our conversation. I was astounded by the honesty, wisdom, and work I observed. I was a humble and grateful witness to Solomon's changing life. I suspected we would return to this issue again. The use and neglect of the Gift was obviously impacting his outlook, bringing him both struggle and hope.

Chapter XII

efore long, things began to change in Jerusalem. Mt. Zion was no longer the depository of supplies to build the great temple of the Lord. It had become a construction site. For years it had simply been a place of preparation and high hopes. It had sat in that condition so long that most had become accustomed to the awkward pending nature of the site. What began in joy seemed headed for disappointment and shame. Many who had walked by grumbling, "I will believe it when I see it," were now praising God, singing a new song.

The earth was slowly and painstakingly being moved, and the huge stones from the quarry were being placed to form the foundation. Workers and craftsmen from many guilds and countries were on site, plying their trades. Solomon, for his part, was communicating the plan of the Lord for this most holy endeavor, as given to him by his father, King David.

Solomon's wisdom was tested during this building project. His involvement as king was to exert no more influence than absolutely necessary, while at the same time neglect no necessary detail. It was a tricky balance that required discerning wisdom. This process not only built a magnificent temple, it developed within Solomon the necessary character for meaningful relationships. In the midst of such a magnificent project, the Gift was never farther than an arm's reach from Solomon.

What was happening on the inside of Solomon was having an astounding effect on the outside world around him. The king began to meet in public before his subjects to judge and counsel the daily dealings of the people with the wisdom of God. His personal approach and application of God's wisdom was remarkable, and it blessed people of all kinds throughout the nation. One such ruling typifies the powerful ministry God's wisdom was having through his servant:

Two women came to the king and stood before him. One of them said, "My lord, this woman and I live in the same house. I had a baby while she was there with me. The third day after my child was born, this woman also had a baby. We were alone; there was no one in the house but the two of us.

"During the night this woman's son died because she lay on him. So she got up in the middle of the night and took my son from my side while I your servant was asleep. She put him by her breast and put her dead son by my breast. The next morning, I got up to nurse my son—and he was dead! But when I looked at him closely in the morning light, I saw that it wasn't the son I had borne."

The other woman said, "No! The living one is my son; the dead one is yours."

But the first one insisted, "No! The dead one is yours; the living one is mine." And so they argued before the king.

The king said, "This one says, 'My son is alive and your son is dead,' while that one says, 'No! Your son is dead and mine is alive.'"

Then the king said, "Bring me a sword." So they brought a sword for the king. He then gave an order: "Cut the living child in two and give half to one and half to the other."

The woman whose son was alive was filled with compassion for her son and said to the king, "Please, my lord, give her the living baby! Don't kill him!"

But the other said, "Neither I nor you shall have him. Cut him in two!"

Then the king gave his ruling: "Give the living baby to the first woman. Do not kill him; she is his mother."

When all Israel heard the verdict the king had given, they held the king in awe, because they saw that he had wisdom from God to administer justice.[xiv]

On another occasion, the king shared his wisdom concerning temperament and perception:

As the king sat in the city gate, a wealthy traveler from the North came inquiring about the hospitality of Jerusalem. The king in turn questioned the traveler, "How did you find the hospitality in Damascus?"

"Oh!" said the traveler, "the city was crowded and rude, accommodations were too modest, food was ill prepared, and the service was awful."

To which the king replied, "I'm so sorry for your treatment, but I'm afraid you are in for more of the same in our city."

The traveler pressed on, wagging his head. About an hour later a merchant also traveling from Damascus asked the same question at the city gate. Solomon responded with the question he had asked earlier, to which the merchant answered, "Old Damascus was beautiful, had wonderful people, welcoming accommodations, and savory food."

The king rejoined, "You are in for greater hospitality here, perhaps the very best of all." The king understood that one's interior state most influences one's external experience.

During one of our conversations, I could not help but affirm the new boldness in which the king was undertaking the temple project and the practical application of God's wisdom displayed among the people of his kingdom.

Solomon confided, "In my travels I met various people on the pathway leading towards God's presence. Some, like the prayer hermits in their caves, sought God in silence and solitude, seeking to be with the Lord in quiet stillness. Others preferred the industry of study, discussion, building, and creating. They too sought the Lord, desiring to do all they could for God's glory.

"As I observed this, I realized the merit of each path but was vexed by its apparent lack of wholeness. One way seemed too isolated and removed from the world. The other seemed so busy and caught up in the world. I considered these thoughts for many days and shared them with a wise rabbi who listened to my dilemma. He counseled that many of our most troubling thoughts find resolution when seemingly conflicting ideas, existing together, form a single truth.

"The rabbi illustrated his assertion by asking me to pick up a stick. As I did, he asked me to carefully observe my action and its implications. I was confused and did not understand the point he was trying to get across until he gestured toward the opposite end of my stick saying, 'You cannot pick up one end of the stick without receiving the other end as well.'

"That is when the insight struck me like a huge bell tolling: life requires both stillness and activity, solitude and community, being and doing to remain in balance. It is tempting to view these things as either or, right versus wrong. However, it is in the balance of the two—meditation and service—that we find a whole way to grow, discern, and live.

"As I sat there with the stick in my hands, it occurred to me that this was, in fact, the power of the Gift. Both the mirror and window caused me to look inward and be with God, which is meditation. In the same instant, they thrust me outward toward my work with others, which is service. Without this unique balance, the Gift itself would be lopsided and useless. Together they merge, creating a double blessing. God's use of the Gift in my life influences me inwardly. At the same time, the Gift sends me out into the world so I may influence people as God's servant.

"Before I left the rabbi, he spoke a word to me I hope to never forget. He said, 'True spirituality, like the stick in your hand, must touch all of your life, or it will touch none of your life.' I believe he was trying to tell me that true wisdom must be allowed to touch me deeply, all of me, if real change is going to take root and flourish.

True spiritual wisdom cannot be selectively applied to only the areas of my life that I choose. It will change all of me or none of me. Likewise, I must set wisdom free in our world if I expect and hope the world to change. I cannot control or direct it; I must let it go. My clever plans and remedies are no match for God's life-changing way."

As I sat and listened to the king, I was struck by the blessing and power of God's presence with us.

CHAPTER XIII

he king's rise was a quick and steep ascent, following in the footsteps of his father, David, the great king. He completed the temple in a remarkable seven years. The walls of the temple rose heavenward as did the wisdom, maturity, and leadership of King Solomon. In fact we were all rising upon the same tide as the glory of the Lord increased in our midst. These were heady days for all the people of Israel.

The Lord's power and glory were made manifest during the time of the temple's dedication. All of Israel had gathered in Jerusalem and the surrounding area for a fourteen day festival of worship, music, dancing, and feasting. During this time, an astonishing twenty-two thousand cattle and a hundred and twenty thousand sheep and goats were sacrificed. At the beginning of the dedication festival, the priests and Levites carried up the Ark of the Covenant. When the priests placed the Ark in the holy place, the temple was filled with a cloud of the Lord's mighty presence and glory.

All the people rose at the presence of the Lord, and the king stood before the altar in front of the whole assembly of Israel and spread out his hands toward heaven and prayed:

"O Lord God of Israel, there is no God like you in heaven above or on earth below—you who keep your covenant of love with your servants who continue wholeheartedly in your way. You have kept your promise to your servant David my father; with your mouth you have promised and with your hand you have fulfilled it—as it is today.

"Now Lord, God of Israel, keep for your servant David my father the promises you made to him when you said, 'You shall never fail

to have a man to sit before me on the throne of Israel if only your sons are careful in all they do to walk before me as you have done. And now, O God of Israel, let your word that you promised your servant David my father come true.

"But will God really dwell on earth? The heavens, even the highest heaven, cannot contain you. How much less this temple I have built! Yet give attention to your servant's prayer and his plea for mercy, O Lord my God. Hear the cry and the prayer that your servant is praying in your presence this day. May your eyes be open toward this temple night and day, this place of which you said, 'My Name shall be there,' so that you will hear the prayer your servant prays toward this place. Hear the supplication of your servant and of your people Israel when they pray toward this place. Hear from heaven, your dwelling place, and when you hear, forgive.

"When they sin against you—for there is not one who does not sin—and you become angry with them and give them over to the enemy, who takes them captive to his own land, far away or near; and if they have a change of heart in the land where they are held captive, and repent and plead with you in the land of their conquerors and say, 'We have sinned, we have done wrong, we have acted wickedly'; and if they turn back to you with all their heart and soul in the land of their enemies who took them captive, and pray to you toward the land you gave their fathers, toward the city you have chosen and the temple I have built for your Name; then from heaven, your dwelling place, hear their prayer and their plea, and uphold their cause. And forgive your people, who have sinned against you; forgive all the offenses they have committed against you, and cause their conquerors to show them mercy; for they are your people and your inheritance, whom you brought out of Egypt, out of that iron-smelting furnace.

"May your eyes be open to your servant's plea and to the plea of your people Israel, and may you listen to them whenever they cry out to you."[xv]

The prayer was extraordinary in several ways. In the presence of the entire assembly, King Solomon spoke plainly to the Lord God, dedicating the temple. On a deeper level, he was dedicating God to the people and the people to God; he filled the distance between us and God like a bridge.

The words of Solomon's prayer surprised me because they were not what I expected. He addressed God as the keeper of the covenant of *love*, rather than the covenant of *law*. The distinction between law and love was not minor, nor did it go unnoticed. The more common covenant of law was expected. Solomon drew on the less common, more relational address—the covenant of love. I heard the effect of the Gift in the king's prayer through his subtle choice of words. The king chose the term of endearment—love—reflecting the Lord God's deepest desire. God's preference was the language of love rather than legal terms and the language of the law.

Through the entire prayer, Solomon begged God to hear his people—not merely hear our words physically, but listen and act on our behalf. Again the intercession was also surprising. Solomon did not ask for blessing, prosperity, or strength to keep the covenant. On behalf of Israel, the king asked the Lord for forgiveness, mercy, and compassion in advance of our inevitable forthcoming sin and unfaithfulness.

Again, the Gift had influenced Solomon's view of our true intended relationship with God. The mirror and the window had revealed to Solomon that we could never be perfect. We could never appease God with our sacrifice, our behavior, or our good works. However, we could walk with God as the Lord's people, trusting God for all things, especially forgiveness. This prayer, inferring that we might relate to God based on God's effort and not our own, was astounding. Thus our relationship to God, the covenant of love, is sustained by God's willingness to show mercy, grant forgiveness, and thus fulfill and keep the covenant. This was all completely amazing!

At the end of the mighty prayer, fire came down from heaven, consuming sacrifices and accepting the king's intercession. The whole assembly fell on their faces at the awesome display of God's glory. Beyond the dedication of the temple so much more was becoming clear. We were beginning to experience our true nature as God's people, relating to one another and God through wisdom. This wisdom was made manifest to the king, just as it had been promised on Mt. Gibeon.

A second extraordinary event took place between God and Solomon privately after the festival of dedication. The Lord appeared to him a second time as he had on the mountain many years ago. This meeting proved to be a stern affirmation of Solomon's prayer. Indeed, the Lord affirmed his covenant relationship with the people—God the perpetual forgiver of a constantly needy and repentant people. However, in a resolute warning, God reminded Solomon that he, like his father David, should also live in daily repentance, seeking the Lord. The Gift that had wisely led him thus far was invaluable to his own continued spiritual legacy and that of his descendants.

The Lord God was making clear who was the Sovereign and who was the servant. As long as Solomon, God's servant, would live out of his deeper self depending on God, his sovereign, Solomon would never bear the consequences of his shallow self, alienated from God.

I marveled at how the humble Gift, a small window and mirror, could keep one so powerfully focused on God, others, and self. I was in awe of the simplicity and practicality of the Gift. I was struck by the far-reaching effect this Gift could have linking a king to his God, while leading a whole nation to the throne room of the divine King.

CHAPTER XIV

hereafter King Solomon continued to grow in wisdom. Strong and quick like a vine in early spring, he flowered and bore fruit. A self-professed man of wisdom came before the king one day to test him before all the people at the city's gate.

He asked, "O great king, on my way up to your beautiful city along the Jericho road I happened upon a crippled beggar beaten, robbed, and left for dead. If there indeed is a wonderful, merciful Almighty, why did he not do something about this terrible injustice?"

"I'm afraid your thinking is clouded, leading you to misunderstand," Solomon replied. "God does care and did reconcile this injustice. God sent you to attend to the beggar. What did you do for him?" All the people were in awe and wonder at the wisdom of their king.

The king's wisdom was not merely limited to his profound spiritual understanding, writing, and magnificent building. The chronicles of the king proclaim:

> *He described plant life, from the cedar of Lebanon to the hyssop that grows out of walls. He also taught about animals and birds, reptiles and fish. Men of all nations came to listen to Solomon's wisdom, sent by all the kings of the world, who had heard of his wisdom.*[xvi]

One such visitor who came was neither a man nor a king. Makeda, Queen of Sheba, Ethiopia, arrived in grand splendor as if from another world. She came in a great caravan of camels carrying spices, gold, and precious stones. We were fascinated by her traditions and customs. From afar Queen Makeda could not comprehend the depth of the king's wisdom nor the breadth of his wealth, so she came to see for herself. She confessed that all she experienced far exceeded what she had been told.

She said to the king, "The report I heard in my own country about your achievements and your wisdom is true. But I did not believe these things until I came and saw with my own eyes. Indeed, not even half was told me; in wisdom and wealth you have far exceeded the report I heard. How happy your men must be! How happy your officials, who continually stand before you and hear your wisdom! Praise be to the Lord your God, who has delighted in you and placed you on the throne of Israel. Because of the Lord's eternal love for Israel, he has made you king, to maintain justice and righteousness."[xvii]

The queen had many questions on her mind, and the king was able to wisely address all her concerns. They also exchanged abundant and lavish gifts. The queen had a life-changing experience with God's wisdom, and her kingdom was dramatically influenced by her visit. It is written:

"King Solomon gave the Queen of Sheba all she desired and asked for, besides what he had given her out of his royal bounty."[xviii]

It was also written that the legendary reputation and renown of the king and his kingdom spread far and wide.

"King Solomon was greater in riches and wisdom than all the other kings of the earth. The whole world sought audience with Solomon to hear the wisdom God had put in his heart."[xix]

During one of our conversations, the king began to expound on what he later called "heart wisdom."

"I carry a burden for people whose approach to God leaves them incomplete, divided from one another and God. One extreme is so consumed with thinking about God that they are paralyzed and rarely act for God. The other extreme is so busy for God, that they have become exhausted and spend little time with God. Anatomically speaking, some overuse their heads, or think, without engaging their hands, while others overuse their hands, or act, without engaging

– 73 –

their minds. Neither extreme can work by itself and is rendered incomplete. Mysteriously, each needs the other for balance and wholeness."

"So, how do you propose we bridge the gap between such extremes?" I asked.

Solomon responded, "Considering our anatomy, let me suggest the neglected organ—the heart. The heart is our spiritual center and is able to mediate between our warring extremes. When we live through our hearts, our lives recognize the need to balance our thinking and acting rather than choosing between them. However, something more important happens in this process. The wisdom of the heart does more than merely balance our thinking and acting. Governed by the heart, both our thinking about God and our acting for God takes on a dramatic shift. Our approach to God is altered from thoughts and deeds for God into a relationship with God. The heart teaches us what God really desires.

"God prefers more than our mental ascent or physical sacrifice. God yearns for us; the Lord enjoys us. God longs for a deep, intimate friendship in which our thinking becomes adoration and our action becomes offering. This change of heart is essential to leaving our shallow, individual selves behind, so we can become our deepening God-gifted selves. Both the mirror and the window are enabling me to see, and I am beginning to understand these matters of the heart. Consider our wonder when we experience the change of a garden grub into a beautiful butterfly. Is not the turning of our hearts toward God by far more important and powerful? The Gift is opening my spiritual eyes and redirecting my focus from my narrow point of view to God's grand and glorious vision."

King Solomon asserted this was why he used the spiritual heart in so much of his wisdom writings. He loved to share examples.

Of the condition of the heart he wrote:

A happy heart makes the face cheerful, but heartache crushes the spirit.[xx]

Concerning his own heart he wrote:

The king's heart is in the hand of the Lord; God directs it like a watercourse wherever he pleases. All a man's ways seem right to him, but the Lord weighs the heart.[xxi]

Applying the heart he wrote:

Apply your heart to instruction and your ears to words of knowledge. My son, if your heart is wise, then my heart will be glad; my inmost being will rejoice when your lips speak what is right.[xxii]

The king attributed all his wisdom discoveries to God, who blessed him with the Gift. The humble old window and mirror granted him an extraordinary view deep into himself, God, and others. As long as the Gift held his gaze, he was able to see as he had never seen before. All of the blessings that touched the life of Solomon blessed so many others as well.

Chapter XV

t this point, I would like to have recorded that our king, his Gift, and the kingdom continued to increase in God's mercy and wisdom. However, dear reader, you are well aware of the confounding twists and turns that life pays out. Solomon's life also followed a crooked path.

One of the unforeseen results of reaching the top of the mountain is that there is simply nowhere else to go. Unless one has received the humble grace and mastered the artful skill of descent, the options for staying on top are few and brutal. Most either die of depleted resources such as food and water, or they carelessly misstep and fall. Like a frightened bear cub high in a forest tree, being on top can leave one stuck and trapped with no place to go.

It took surprisingly few years before King Solomon became ensnared. Blinded by the glorious view from the top of his world, he neglected or forgot the Gift that had helped him attain the summit. I suspect that somewhere along the way the king's custom of reaching for the Gift was interrupted; and in the thrill and momentum of success, he failed to return to his habit. You may ask, "How do you know?" Well, in truth, I did not know for sure until sometime later. But this is what I observed at the time.

Solomon not only inherited the fortune of King David, he also began to amass his own wealth as well. Through his business dealings and gifts from visitors, his resources grew and multiplied. I believe the accumulated wealth and power associated with it began to deceive Solomon into thinking that his own intellect, cunning, and common sense were the main reasons for his success. As you will recall, God had communicated a very different vision for the king: all of Solomon's wealth and power were to be a divine gift in response to the king's humble petition for wisdom. Riches and power, however, have been the undoing of many great ones. Solomon was not the first nor would he be the last to forget the source of his authority, insight, and treasure.

Solomon, like his father, also acquired a weakness for women, too many women. In time, it was reported that the king had seven hundred wives as well as three hundred concubines. Succumbing to this behavior obviously bound him in moral failure with its destructive effect on all his relationships: God, family, and the people of his kingdom.

The king's multiple nuptials with the daughters of neighboring kings doubled as peace treaties. Thus Solomon sought peace through his own means rather than trusting in God's protection. These marriages introduced further corrosive influences over Solomon. The foreign wives brought their false gods with them to Jerusalem. The effects of these gods negatively influenced the already vulnerable king and overpowered him. Solomon's single-hearted devotion to God became divided.

Solomon managed to keep up his kingly appearance. I began to see him differently, however, fraying like an overused rope. He seemed unable or unwilling to survive his own success. As Solomon's shallow self reasserted its own authority, a larger fissure between the king and his God emerged. With the Gift apparently out of sight and reach, Solomon had no ally with which to oppose his insurgent, shallow self. This left the king's deep self weak and wounded, unable to compensate without God's viewpoint through the Gift. Solomon's wisdom began to evaporate. The Gift kept the king connected with God and others, the source and influence of his true wisdom and whole self. Now, however, the king appeared to be going his own way. He seemed to prefer his isolation and was increasing in defensive pride, attempting to do everything on his own. Solomon needed his Gift more than he realized.

Consequently, the ongoing conversations we had both enjoyed

so much became irregular, then dwindled to nothing. For my part, all I could do was wait, hope, and pray. I considered all the ways I could help the king, but without his invitation, I was powerless to intervene. I too was learning to trust in the Lord God's power, even in the face of my king's devastation and the kingdom's demise.

As I witnessed Solomon's slow-motion fall, I noticed two stirrings in my heart. I first considered my king. *How could this happen?* After such great victories and accomplishments, Solomon seemed to be undone by obvious temptations and known dangers. Why was he making such poor decisions? I was frustrated with the feeling of powerlessness. I alone could not "save" the king.

I also was angry with the king. *How could he do this?* Solomon's own wisdom came to mind, "Unguarded strength becomes a double portion of weakness." Secondly, this caused me to consider my own life. I likewise walked dangerously close to the cliff's edge at times. Could not my unchecked blind spots lead to my own downfall and self-destruction? I am so exact in pinpointing the faults of others. Why is it so easy to detect in others what I find so difficult to see in myself?

In the midst of observing my king's undoing, I became aware of my own modernity. I had outlived one king, would I outlive another? How could I know? My activities had become restricted to writing and waiting—waiting on the king and waiting to die. Days had turned to years since I had last been with the king in conversation. There were simply no occasions to get close to the king to see how he was doing.

Eventually, a servant of the king knocked at my door saying, "The king will now see you," as if our last appointment had been just days ago. I had been hoping for just this kind of opportunity. However, the sudden timing caught me off guard. In fact, I sensed the presence of great fear and doubt within, not knowing how all this would turn out. All I could do was go and see.

The king's appearance had changed dramatically. The man now

sitting before me on his familiar, ornate throne had somehow shrunk in size, stature, and attitude. His hair had grayed and thinned. His body stooped as if caving in on itself. His once bright eyes seemed dull, encircled in darkness, nervously darting around the room.

Gone was the king's strong composure, leaving him weak and fidgety. His voice was a mixture of fatigue, anger, and desperation. He looked like a man who knew too much and did not like it. He was both guarded and explosive, like a wounded animal. His life was dilapidated and shattered, as a ruined wall around a conquered city.

I was shocked by what I saw. The vision left me unbalanced and disoriented. Before me was the same king who once commanded my submission, even reverence. I attempted to gather myself, fearful that my face had already betrayed my surprise. Frantically I forced my mind to come up with something to say, some place to begin. Solomon had already begun our conversation. Sensing some relief, I began to listen.

"All is vanity," he asserted defiantly. I had the profound sense he now considered me his accuser rather than his companion.

"What do you mean, vanity?" I responded.

The king persisted, "Everything is vain, all I have worked for, all I have and all I am, it is all meaningless, as if trying to catch the wind."

At that point the king's voice began to elevate into a tirade, bouncing from one subject to the next. I worked at staying calm, attentively listening.

"I devoted myself to wisdom, its study and exploration, only to be disappointed, finding it merely a heavy if not impossible burden laid upon man. Much wisdom only increases one's sorrow and grief. Not only that, but like the fool, so too the wise will die."

The king continued, "So I sought out pleasure, I denied myself nothing my body craved. Yet, it too was meaningless and the consequences for my actions are a tremendous burden, a moral debt from which I will never be free. All of it was evil. So again I reversed course, working hard to be industrious. I built and amassed a great fortune, but this too was meaningless. For all I have I will not always possess. I too will someday perish, and into other hands it will go, and I will no longer enjoy it. No matter how hard I try, what I do and where I go will all be worthless. There is nothing new under the sun, all is vanity and meaningless."

At what seemed like a point of exhaustion while the king seemed to catch his breath, I asked, "Where is God in all of this? Where is the God of the mountain and the temple who spoke to you of great promises extending the covenant to you?"

It did not take the king long to respond. "Yes! Yes! God," Solomon snapped, "God places eternity in our hearts, but who can understand it? Not I! God demands my fear, my respect, and somehow I will, I must! However, I fail to understand the point. This is chasing after the wind. So I will stand in awe of God, and try to be careful with what I say and do. However, God does not enable me to enjoy the life I have created for myself, and this is grievous in my sight.

"I did enjoy God in my younger days, I will admit, before these latter days of trouble. Back then, I taught with enthusiasm and hope to fear God, keep the commands, knowing that God will bring judgment. Today, I believe it only in despair. I suppose I must believe in God."

The king crossed his arms and sat strangely satisfied as if his statements had settled some long standing score. I had the sense that while the king did indeed fear God, he seemed more afraid. He was obviously disappointed and angry at God for how his life had turned out. Solomon's ranting conveyed the image of God being responsible for all that had gone wrong, yet powerless to help him or bring real meaning to his life. According to Solomon's testimony, God was merely worthy of blame, not blessing. Solomon seemed to bitterly accuse God, like the son of an abusive father. Time, the pressure of the kingdom, and the king's poor choices had conspired to undo the man who once held the very promises of God in his own right hand.

We sat motionless staring at each other. He looked so lost behind his bluster and false confidence. I was afraid, afraid to breathe much less talk; what could I say? How could I answer the king? There was a final question—one I did not know whether I could or should ask. As I debated this in my mind I decided I must pursue it.

I said, "O King, what has become of the Gift? The Gift of God, passed down by the fathers to your father, King David?"

Solomon's shocked expression and watery eyes shot an evil gaze that struck icy terror within me. I felt cold like one exposed on the slopes of Mt. Hermon in the dead of winter. In his eyes, I saw a lifetime of pain, anger, frustration, sorrow, and even regret. It was also a knowing gaze; he understood my inquiry. After a long, intense silence, the king gave a defiant answer to my question. He turned his face to the wall and enclosed himself in a tomb of silence.

CHAPTER XVI

hile he was keeping his self-imposed silence, King Solomon's influence continued to diminish. He did not merely avoid me; he sealed off the whole kingdom beyond his door. His once beautiful palace was becoming the dark dungeon of his soul.

I also withdrew into my own world of doubt and wondered what had happened. This continued as the burning question of my heart. *Why did my successful king, guided by the Gift, stumble over the same Gift?* I considered how Solomon's disregard for his Gift had become his intolerable burden. I asked myself the question, *Why do I squander hope, opportunity, or blessing? What is it about me that defiantly rejects the help I need, and in failure, consider myself the noble martyr for doing so?*

I later learned that the king devoted much of his silence to considering my final question from our previous conversation. It took a while, but the king's uneasy conscience, his active mind, and the lapse of time conspired to move his heart. Not wishing to appear too eager, he subtly made his interest known in continuing our conversation. In the king's timing, we were once again face to face.

When I saw the king and sat with him, it felt as though the king's silence had not been merely defensive isolation. The silence appeared to soften him; his attitude and countenance seemed less rigid and hostile. I noticed a hunger or perhaps a longing within him. He gave the impression of a very lost and lonely man stumbling home, fumbling at making amends.

Our conversation took on the decided tone of confession. This topic was uncomfortable for both of us. No doubt, baring his heavy soul must have been humiliating for this powerful king. Becoming the king's confessor was intimidating and rather overwhelming for me. After all, who was I?

The weight of difficulty in this conversation also hinted at the hope of healing and reconciliation for us. I believe Solomon needed to hear his own voice shatter his gloom with words of remorse that might allow in some light.

I needed to receive his confession, not as a superior but as a companion and a listener, hearing with humble ears of compassion. Surrounding us was the presence of God guiding, protecting, and leading, as a mother attending to her children. It was both an awkward and awesome event, a holy moment. I heard extraordinary words, ones rarely spoken out loud.

The king began, "I am still astounded and unnerved by the fact that my life could be so wonderful, only to end up in this horrendous mess. What you already know, Zadok, must become plain to others; I have used every blessing offered by God to serve my own ends: wisdom, wealth, the kingdom itself, and my very life.

"I have failed everyone, beginning with God, the wife of my youth, my children, my friends, and the leaders and subjects of the kingdom. I have twisted every relationship in order to satisfy myself. All my plans to bring God glory eventually turned to praise for me. Even the things I did well for a time I fouled and corrupted like an overused spring or watering hole.

"I am attempting to confess before you this day, Zadok, because you are my priest. You know my heart and you know the crooked path I have chosen. I repent this day not merely of all I have done, but also what I have left undone. I repent of who I have become.

"God promised me a life of wisdom because that is what I sought. God gave me the Gift so that I could know the way, and so much more besides. Yet, Zadok, despite all this provision and blessing, I have become instead an unwise man. Humiliated, my life has become an abomination, the consummation of wisdom's counterpart. I have lived a lie, not a life. I started well, but I have stumbled and fallen so far."

The king sat in silence for a moment as if gathering strength to move forward, collecting his thoughts and picking his words carefully. I too used the cover of silence, considering how I might add to the conversation. In that moment, the silence was choosing us and speaking to us in a way deeper than words.

King Solomon continued, "I have become the king in name only. In reality, I have been the thief of the kingdom, pilfering from God and my subjects. I have been a fake and a fraud, hiding my base motive behind a pious appearance. I abandoned God privately first and then publicly. I sought my own agenda, attempting to satisfy the appetites of my flesh. I ran the nation to serve myself, not its people, let alone God. I used religion to glorify the king, not the Lord. I was thoughtless and selfish. I have caused so much hurt and pain for those I supposedly loved, driving many away, cutting the rest off. I was a hireling among those I was called to shepherd and love; I carelessly scattered the flock.

"With my head crammed with facts and knowledge, I believed I knew better than anyone else. I believed my big head would provide the wisdom I needed, but my heart was as empty as a whistle. I was unbalanced and lopsided, unable to discern true wisdom.

"I spent many years fooling myself. I was persuaded that I had outgrown the Gift; somehow I had mined all its wisdom, plumbed all its depths, thereby preparing me to face the world on my own. To the degree that I accepted my silly reasoning, the more I became confused. I walked away from the Gift when I needed it most. What is worse, the more hints I received about my perilous condition, the more I turned a deaf ear to those life-correcting revelations. Pretending to know and to see my situation only increased my blindness. I completely disregarded the window and mirror of wisdom's true vision.

"During this continuous downward spiral, my shallow self rose to uproot and overtake the deep self that had been planted in my heart. Without my Gift, I was as defenseless as a walled city without gates. I am just understanding how cunningly the shallow self can reemerge like an underground river that reappears as a raging torrent, more powerful than before. I had willingly given myself to it, diving in head first. I became absorbed and overcome in the swift current of deception.

"Once I began to perceive my perilous condition and the widespread consequences of my calamity, I tried to right things myself. I was a desperate man in need of help. Yet, I destructively determined to make it on my own; but this was futile, so I lashed out in another direction.

"When all else failed and crumbled around me, I decided that my troubles were God's fault. In my sick heart, God was too small to bless, yet big enough to blame. I made it my aim to make God the scapegoat, excusing myself from all that was wrong. My upside-down logic told me that my solution was my problem, and my help was my enemy. So I avoided the help of everyone. I sensed an arrogant satisfaction and superiority by casting God and others in the bad light of my sick interpretations.

"I felt strangely justified in my accusations and blaming. I loved my martyrdom and clung to it as a badge of honor. As I saw it, I was the one entitled to vindication, and all others deserved blame. After all, God had let me down, and everyone else was jealous of my wisdom, power, wealth, and success. I was forsaken. I was betrayed by everyone else. I sought the attention of others so I could in turn spit it back in their face.

"Having run off most of my family and friends, squarely pinning the blame on them, no one was left to hate but myself. So, it did not take long for me to find and set off down that path. I came to hope that hating myself could become some kind of penance for my wrongdoing. I coveted punishment for my waywardness. I exalted my errors in yet another attempt to pay my own way, eliminate my debt, make it right, proving I could do it myself. I had discovered my last pleasure in life, pity, feeling sorry for my self-inflicted wounds. In the guise of mourning my past errors, I was actually nursing them. Yet all of this was again a futile exercise in deception.

"Zadok, I have been completely wrong about everything, compounded by my conceited claims to know it all. I am sorry and completely mortified. In my sin I have disobeyed God, dishonored my family, ruined all my relationships, and wasted my life. I feel guilty beyond forgiveness, hopeless of any redeemable future. I am bitterly ashamed. I would do anything to alter or reverse my tragic circumstances. I fear no help is available for me. I have dug my hole so deep I cannot see any way to get out. I sense my life is veiled by a shroud of sadness so thick I can no longer see my way. This sadness lingers like a vile taste in my mouth.

"Dear Zadok, your difficult but simple question concerning the Gift has struck a nerve I thought completely and forever seared. What about the Gift? There is something in that poignant question that I do not wish to face, but it will not let me go. I feel drawn to the light of its opportunity but am afraid of being consumed by the heat of its fire. For better or worse, I feel a strange compulsion to somehow someway examine your inquiry and locate its true response in my heart. It may well be the last decent thing I am able to do."

With these last words the king hung his head, closed his eyes, and became silent. I knew the confession had ended, so I quietly excused myself. In a somber mood, I walked thoughtfully through the majestic palace and courts on the way back to my cell, considering our conversation. I desperately wanted to believe I had witnessed the king make a turn. *Was this wishful thinking? How could I know?* I thought I noticed the angry, bitter king become a remorseful man full of sorrow. *Was this wreck of a person the once great teacher finding his way? Could he become teachable again? Would the king's distilled sorrow lead him to rich inspiration?* Life yields many lessons—how to do things right, how to do things wrong, and how to survive both.

Chapter XVII

After his confession, the king once again became scarce. I prayed that he was considering our conversation and not returning to spiritual exile. So I gave the king plenty of time and room. What else could I do?

Before too long, we were sitting together, preparing for our conversation. As usual, we sat for a time in silence before we engaged.

Solomon began, "I have been doing a lot of thinking and reflecting on our last conversation."

"Reflection," I responded, "what are you noticing?"

"I am noticing a change of heart, I believe. The confession was a start, a first step, in being truly honest with myself. I have also been dealing with your question. The short answer is that I have picked up the Gift and am using it again."

There was an emotional pause, and I saw tears welling up in his eyes. I asked, "Can you tell me about your tears?"

The king nodded in affirmation and slowly began to speak. "I am feeling so much these days, deep feelings. A great deal of sadness mixed with joy and a glimmer of hope is growing slowly within me. The emotion stems from all I have been learning about the Gift . . . my fall . . . and my ongoing life."

"Your ongoing life," I said hopefully, "sounds very full. What has that been like for you?"

"It has nearly overwhelmed me," the king conceded. "My confession was just the beginning of my process. I had naively assumed I could make a verbal, albeit contrite, confession and everything would be okay, returning back to normal. Well, it has not happened according to plan. As I now see it, I am being drawn toward something deeper . . . a much needed reconciliation."

"Reconciliation," I repeated, "tell me more."

"Well, to begin with," continued the king, "I am being reconciled to myself and my own feelings. As I have said, I began seeking the easy way out of my situation. I was focused on the trouble I was in and not the truth that was being revealed. I felt if I could just make it all go away, things would get better. I still had not come to terms with the fact that I could not fix this mess. You see, my life was demonstrating without a doubt that I was unable to manage it. Even my best efforts were making my problems worse. I was unable to see because I was standing in my own light. Was not all my striving truly vain and futile?"

I nodded in agreement.

"This led me to examine my deeper feelings concerning my confession, which revealed a valuable insight. While I was sorry for all the harm I had caused and the people I had hurt, this was not my primary feeling. I came to realize I was more upset about being caught than being wrong. As king, I resented being found out and exposed for the obvious fraud I had been. I was sorrier for myself than for anyone or anything else. My main concern was still me, my reputation, and how I looked as king.

"As I refocused I began to sense my feelings for those whom I had injured and all the evil I had done. At this point, my confession began to ring true, feeling believable. This is still very difficult for me to face and admit . . ."

"This sounds very powerful," I encouraged.

"I also needed to be reconciled to my motives. Did my intentions match my deeds? Did my high ideals outweigh my actions? What were my motives? I was reminded of a riddle I heard in my youth. A wise man told the story, 'Five birds are sitting in a tree. One of them decides to fly away. How many birds are left?'"

"After thinking about the riddle I replied, 'four.'"

"'No,'" replied the wise man, "'there are five. Deciding to fly and actually flying are two very different things.'

"I had been deceiving myself for a very long time: thinking good thoughts, making big promises, using the right words, all with good intentions—yet, my actions did not match. Intentions are completely powerless without the deeds that back them up. I began to realize there is no real difference between me and my well-intended plans and a person with absolutely no plans if I neglect to take action. In my disregard of the mirror and window, I have noticed I judge myself by my intentions, while I judge others by their deeds. I see what I want, not what is real. This now must change.

"I also needed to be reconciled to my harmful behaviors. I had to consider my responsibility for my actions and inactions. I had conceded all that had happened was a grave mistake, for which I was very sorry indeed. However, this reasoning was too shallow. There was something more. I felt a deeper obligation. Then one evening I picked up the Gift and examined it. I recalled your detailed instruction concerning the use of the Gift and the temptations therein, and the power of your words returned to me like a splash of cold water in my face! You warned me not to be reckless with the Gift, but I had not listened.

"Let us suppose you warned me to stay out of the woods for fear I could get lost or hurt, but I go into the woods anyway. As I enter the forest, I pass signs warning me not to enter. I continue and, of course, something dreadful occurs. Whatever happens at that point could never be considered an accident or a mistake. It must be considered a choice, a foolish but informed choice. My neglect of the Gift and the devastating consequences are no different for me. I have made choices, very poor and costly choices. These were not merely mistakes that I could simply justify with an apology. I have been blatantly and painfully wrong and in some cases intentionally evil.

"No amount of penance or self-hatred can ever change what has happened. However, I can take responsibility for my choices and behaviors; I can seek forgiveness, perform restitution, and make amends with those I have hurt. As I do my part with others, it is essential I trust in God for my own reconciliation, healing, and restoration. I admit I do not have all the answers. I am even fearful of repeating many of the same mistakes. But this I know: I must give up what I have been to become what I could be . . ." The king's voice trailed off into silence.

In a few moments I inquired, "What is stirring in you now?"

After another brief silence the king began again. "As I have told you, I am using the Gift again. I see through the Gift a new vision of God, others, and myself. This leads me to you, dear friend, my priest and companion. I want to thank you for your listening heart. You resisted the temptation to hold my hand in pity or raise your fist in confrontation. You spoke the truth to me in love.

"You did not try to change me; you gave me room enough to dig my own pit, deep and dark. You did not try to rescue me; you offered me space to lift my head from the darkness. You did not try to persuade or advise me; you stepped back and let me stand up. You did not shield me; you allowed me to sense the full intensity of the convicting light and recognize my own dark shadow. You were there each step of the way, in body and spirit. I am eternally grateful, Zadok, for you, your life, and your presence in my life."

As I considered Solomon's affirmation, I silently rejoiced. Peace filled my heart as I reflected on how much could be gained when I held my tongue and freed my ears to simply listen.

Later that evening we concluded our amazing conversation. As I gazed upon the face of my king, which I had beheld from birth, I recalled a proverb he wrote as a young man, "As water reflects a face, so a man's heart reflects the man."[xxiii]

With great satisfaction, I was once again gratified to receive wisdom through Solomon's words and life.

Chapter XVIII

hroughout the remaining years of Solomon's life, he grew in the mercy and forgiveness that was granted him. However, the consequences of his neglecting the Gift prevented him a full return to his former glory and set the kingdom's course toward a tragic future. We, however, resumed our regular conversations, with the Gift being the focus and center of our discussions. The king's heart continued to soften. He became a humbler and gentler man.

Solomon's wisdom returned and increased. I recognized an insightful look in his eyes as he began to find his voice again. In those final years, he neither spoke in public nor committed his wisdom to writing. For the most part, his wisdom was confined to our conversations. These were redeeming and fruitful years for the king and the kingdom, occasionally marred by past regrets and fleeting notions of what might have been.

Some years later, the aging king sought a favor. He said, "I have been meditating on some thoughts as my summary of God's wisdom. I desire to share these thoughts with you, some family, and a few close friends. I would be pleased if you might record my observations."

"As you desire, my king." I was thrilled at the opportunity to see and hear the king teach once again as he had done in days gone by.

When all had gathered, Solomon began, "When people seek to build their own houses of wisdom and so become the spiritual living temple of God, they must erect seven pillars—two pillars set close up front, forming the doorway to wisdom and four pillars to stake out the diameter, which serves to contain the wisdom. The final pillar stands alone in the very center of the house. It holds everything together, bearing the full weight of wisdom. These pillars are the trees of wisdom rooted deep in the soil of God and reaching high into the sky of life.

"The superior seven pillar structure is widely known and used today. However, foolish builders prefer shortcuts, which can yield disastrous results. It is the same with wisdom; the seven pillars are available to all who take the time to attend to them. However, the sluggard who seeks the quick way to wisdom embarks on the fool's path. In doing so, he forsakes wisdom altogether by refusing and resisting the seven pillars.

"Hence, I say that wisdom cries out to you; she is calling your name. Wisdom is making her word known to you in the streets, in the market, in your home, from the temple, and from deep within your heart. Seek wisdom, hear it, receive it, keep it, and guard it. True wisdom is greater than silver or gold. To hear the voice of God and incline your ear to that voice is the beginning of wisdom. This wisdom brings hope to the heart of everyone. No matter what happens in all of life, the holder of God's wisdom will never be put to shame.

"So how does wisdom work? Wisdom, you see, turns your heart toward God as I found in the mirror and window. Once we are facing God, we begin to change just as gold becomes pure in the heat of the crucible. Our lives become pure as we live face to face with God. Before God, our shallow selves begin to dissolve; our deceit, our crooked secrets, our foolishness, and our sins begin to melt in God's presence. Our shallow selves cannot withstand the holy heat of God.

"At the same time, our deep selves are revealed, increasing in truth, compassion, character, and honesty. God's Word and presence begin to fill our lives. This is the ever expanding way of God's wisdom in our hearts. This is what we live for. This wisdom is the hope and long sought home that all wandering humanity seeks. This is the home I hope you will build with the seven pillars."

After this brief introduction, the king began his discourse on the seven pillars of wisdom, as I have transcribed according to the king's request.

"The first two pillars mark the doorpost of wisdom through which all must pass.

"Pillar #1: *Make peace with who you are.*

"When you despise and ignore who you are, wisdom is refused. However, when receiving yourself, wisdom is embraced. We must hold the mirror to our faces, gazing into our own eyes with mercy and wonder. As we do, we will see what is crooked—our shallow selves, and what is upright—our deep selves. As we lovingly learn to face and work with all we see in ourselves, wisdom grows in our souls. The law commands that we love God and neighbors as ourselves. We must therefore love ourselves.

"Loving who we are does not mean overlooking our foolish and deceptive ways. That is why we use the mirror to search for what is both righteous and twisted. As we accept all of who we are, we rejoice in all that is good and hopeful. We also sidestep the snare of one who toils at attempting to look blameless. He loses his battle with concealing deceit, exhausted and frustrated.

"I knew I was beginning to find peace with myself when I was able to admit to blaming others and giving my excuses. Reckoning with our shallow selves is our starting point. Our deeper selves receive this painful but truthful admission, opening the way of wisdom's true and lasting change. Change is the other post, framing the doorway to wisdom.

"Pillar #2: *Yield to the way of change.*

"The change we seek is more desirable than change imposed. A word of unsought advice is like the thrust of a sword. People who lean on their own understanding have slipped from wisdom's path. They cannot change; they can only fall. Here is what I have learned about change: we cannot act as if change is unnecessary, stubbornly wait for change to arrive, or pursue change like a thief. We simply cannot demand change from ourselves or others. Change is a slow, deliberate course like a long river running to the sea.

"The wisdom of making peace with ourselves reveals the entrance to the good path that leads to change. Consider the following three steps along the path. First, change will only take place when we understand its necessity and desire it. When we accept and desire the need for change, our eyes become open to seeing how change works. As this need arises in our hearts, we respond as a thirsty traveler welcomes a cool spring along the trail.

"Next, notice that change is difficult and will appear menacing. Change is always a threat to the shallow self who resists the work and discomfort of change. The window and the mirror enable the deeper self to see what opportunities and blessings change can bring. Focusing on this view of change bears sweet fruit for those who give themselves to it.

"Finally, note that the process of change cannot be complete by simply abandoning former habits, filthy talk, or wicked deeds. The way of wise change is complete through replacement. This is to say that true change occurs when something new takes the place of the old, redeeming and restoring that person's life. Therefore, if I focus on good thoughts, in time I forget to think evil. If I look upon another with compassion and forgiveness, I will lose my anger and resentment. Following the example from the first pillar, I knew I was beginning to change when, without shame, I accepted being wrong. I no longer needed to blame others or make excuses for myself; I changed.

"The next four pillars define the dimensions that contain the wisdom within you.

"Pillar #3: *Allow failure and difficulty to teach you.*
"Failure is a wise teacher and leads you to seek the help you need. Success can lead to a hollow victory that makes you appear right in your own eyes. However, bearing a heavy heart can prompt you to seek wisdom, the pathway of life. When failure and difficulty are recognized as teachers, it can be life changing. It can even cause the

sluggard to go to work, the arrogant to rethink, and the fool to become wise.

"The reproof of failure and difficulty seeks to guide you back on course, not bring shame to the bereft. The window will reveal these teachers, and the mirror will reflect the concealed response of your heart. If you reject these teachers of wisdom, life will become filled with excuses that you whisper to yourself, blame that you place on others, and curses that you speak against God. All this leads you to a life of shame and resentment. There is a way that seems right to a man, but it ends in disappointment. The Lord supplies peculiar teachers; they incline your heart to learn from them. This is the way of wisdom."

Being in the presence of King Solomon as he taught was powerful. His eyes were bright, his hand gestured the way, and his voice was full of conviction and authority.

"Pillar #4: *Open your ears.*

"Consider this fourth pillar in light of the first three.

"How can you make peace with who you are if you cannot listen to your life? How will you ever change if you cannot hear what is wrong or be encouraged by words of hope? How will you truly learn from failure and difficulty if you refuse to hear their wise words of reproof?

"Listening may be the most valuable of human senses when seeking wisdom. Time spent looking through the window and at the mirror of real life will enlarge our compassion and desire for greater listening. Many of the greatest problems in our world and in our lives stem from misunderstanding. Men have gone to battle over mistaken words and careless listening. Words misspoken or falling on deaf ears are like a mouth full of gravel.

"Practice listening. Listen to yourself. Do you know what your own words sound like? Listen to others. Do you hear what they say to you? Do you understand them? Meditate on this. Those who listen to us best influence us the most. They speak wisdom out of an abundance of their hearing.

When our words are many, our ears are stopped and our speech is foolish. When our words are few, our ears are open and our speech is wise.

Not love?

"*Pillar #5: Be obedient—the root of all wisdom.*

"The roots of wisdom run deep. You rarely see the roots of a healthy plant. The root forms the necessary invisible support for production of fruit. We would not see a beautiful flower without its unseen root. Many people today mistake knowledge and education for wisdom. Knowledge and education are always very important, but at the root, obedience must be present. Wisdom is not simply what we know—it is what we do with what we know. Wisdom turns true understanding into righteous holy living.

"Sadly, too many people who consider themselves wise know more than they are willing to obey. Therefore, the wise in heart will embrace obedience, but a chattering fool will not and comes to ruin. The evil deeds of a wicked man ensnare him; the cords of his sin hold him fast. He will die for lack of obedience, led astray by his own great folly.

"Our God desires more from us than submission to laws, deeds, and sacrifice. God longs for a relationship of trust and love. This is the word of the Lord, God's appeal to you:

> *My sons and daughters, keep my words by your obedience deep inside. Keep my commands by the way you live. Guard my teaching by making me the apple of your eye. Bind my love to your fingers and write my will on the tablet of your heart.*[xxiv]

"For you see, a wise person does not reflect nor reveal oneself in the mirror and window. Wise children actually reveal the God who makes them wise. Others will be drawn to God through our obedience.

"Pillar #6: *Love others by giving wisdom away.*

"The wisdom that reveals God to the world is God loving the world through us. What good is wisdom if it does not love? A wisdom that sounds and appears upright but does not love, hurts others and is not wise. It is like a sharp thorn on the path. Such a thorn pierces the sandal, easily going swift and deep into a man's foot.

"As you have received great love into your heart, remember to give it away freely through your hands. Then you will find favor and a good name in the sight of God and man. When we do not love others, our mirror and window will reveal that we neither love God nor ourselves. How can the water of our household benefit us when our well is bitter? Can it be shared with others? In the same way, do not withhold good from those who ask. When you can bless, do so. This is the wisdom of love.

"Love not only changes our heart, it changes the heart of the beloved as well. Love can overpower hatred and evil. For, you see, hatred stirs dissension, but love overtakes all wrongs. Even loving our enemies makes us more like God and less like an enemy. Can we love too much? Can too much love make us foolish? As you would carefully weigh your gold on a scale, place on the scale the love that God has given you, then balance the scale with the same amount of love for others. This is the measure that pleases God, blesses others, and makes you wise and free."

As the king addressed the final pillar, the centerpiece and load bearing support for his house of wisdom, I observed a change. His tone was more personal, his passion intensified. The expression on his face brightened, brimming with joy and hope. The old king paused for a moment of silence—maybe praying, resting, or both—then continued.

"Pillar #7: *Know the difference between the Giver and the Gift.*

"Understanding the true nature of the Gift is the most profound wisdom I believe I will ever learn. For most of my life I misunderstood, or should I say misidentified the Gift. I believed I held the Gift in my hands, that I used the small mirror and window as the Gift itself. Certainly God had given me the purse and its contents, but only as props—mere illustrations of the Gift. In reality, it only pointed in the direction of the true Gift—God. The mystery of God defies human understanding. In fact, what cannot be said about God will always be greater than what can be said. But this is what I have learned.

"God is my Gift. God has given me life and all my days. The Lord's life-giving aim is to guide and nurture my deep self. My shallow self has fought and continues to fight me by blurring my vision, twisting my emotions, and ransacking my reason, all of this in an effort to distort God's simple but powerful wisdom. God does not merely give us the gift of love. *God is the Gift*, and love is expressed in God's giving. When I focus on God, my Gift, I am filled with God, and my life manifests God's image. I learn to forget my old ways, the people I am angry with, and how to feel sorry for myself. Pity, personal grievances, judgments, striving, and grim determination begin to fade. All this is being replaced with love, hope, humility, honesty, confidence, and peace.

"I have spent much of my life burdened, thinking I needed to be more than I was. So I tried hard to be the wisest man, the greatest builder, and the most powerful king. Then a few years ago, the Lord gave me a healing dream, a new vision of myself with Him. In the dream I went to meet with the Almighty. I was deeply troubled, afraid the Lord would ask, 'Why were you not like your father, King David?' Instead, the Lord God surprised me by asking, 'Why were you not simply King Solomon?' The dream changed the way I thought and felt about myself and God.

"It is dawning on me with every new day that I need God more than anything God could ever give me. God is the One who heals me, sets me free, and calls my deep self to emerge out of my shallow self. God has created everything in life to lead us forward on the spiritual path: good times or bad, blessings or curses, illness or health, poverty or fortune, power or weakness, love or hatred, friends or enemies. Each of these conditions or characters presents unique opportunities to find God our Gift, serve our neighbor, and live at peace with ourselves. God is the Giver and the Gift. Knowing, being, and operating in God's presence is the Gift that brings meaning to life; this is life itself.

"I count myself fortunate to be learning what we all must know. God is always waiting for us like a mother who is waiting and expecting the homecoming of her wayward child. This simple but powerful picture buried deep in our hearts may be the wisest image our mind's eye can ever see."

Solomon closed with a gentle warning, "Forsake not these seven pillars of wisdom. Take time to name and acknowledge them. In doing so, they will guide you to God, reminding you of true wisdom, and you will be encouraged. Your shallow self that exhibits laziness, doubt, and desire for control will conspire within you to neglect them. Its untrustworthy voice will attempt to deceive you into thinking that the seven pillars are impossible, too demanding, and too revealing. This voice says the pillars are not wisdom; they are stumbling blocks.

"But I say to you, the seven pillars are stepping stones, not stumbling blocks; walk in the way they will lead you. This is the narrow way of honesty and humility leading to God and becoming your deeper self."

At the close of Solomon's discourse, I had no way of knowing this would be the last time I would hear my king's voice. I sat motionless. I was in awe of the king's life and wisdom. It occurred to me that I was in the presence of a man who had received God as his Gift, blessed his neighbor as his beloved, and accepted himself as true after all.

Chapter XIX

he night was short. Very early the next morning, I was awakened to the sound of knocking at my door. I was reminded of that first alarming knock a lifetime ago.

The king's attendant said, "King Solomon, son of the great King David, has died and been gathered to his fathers this day in the city of Jerusalem. Preparations are now underway." As the attendant turned to leave, he looked over his shoulder, as if seeking permission to add something. I gave a slight nod.

The attendant continued, "I saw something rather strange and feel compelled to say something to someone. May I tell you?"

"Yes," I consented.

"I found the king this morning in his chamber. He was lying on his back in bed. While approaching, I noticed a worn, silk purse at the foot of his bed. As I came alongside the king, I saw in his right hand a small framed mirror, and in his left a window of the same size." The attendant then told me he placed the two items in the bag, as that seemed the right thing to do, then deposited the bag somewhere in the king's treasury. He confided that he had told no one of these peculiar findings in the king's chamber.

I affirmed his actions with a knowing smile and a hand on his shoulder, and he turned and left my room without another word.

Like most great treasures, they have either been lost or are so well hidden that we shall never find them. I assume this to be the fate of the purse containing the small window and mirror. However, I, Zadok, priest of the great kings of Israel, declare that as it is God's will that the word of the Torah be buried deep within the hearts of every man, woman, and child; the same must be true of the Gift, finding a home in every human heart. I believe that God's self-giving Gift reveals that we too may truly know and love God, others, and ourselves just as Solomon did with his mirror and window. In so doing, others will see God through us like a window as we see God in ourselves through a mirror.

Many mysteries yet remain for those who would seek God, the Living Gift and Eternal Wisdom, but in this threefold command I remain utterly confident:

> "*Love the Lord your God with all your heart and with all your soul and with all your strength and with all your mind; and, love your neighbor as yourself.*"[xxv]

JOURNEY'S
END

✠

CHAPTER XX

s Abba MeKonen closes the Book of Zadok, he stands up, turning toward the Holy of Holies, and bends at the waist for a moment of silence and adoration. The moment feels like an eternity, my mind racing.

What did I just spend the day listening to? Was this actually an ancient text, perhaps a "lost" volume of the Old Testament? What about this book's message and wisdom? How could I obtain a copy for future work and study? What should I do next?

I could see the shadows in the room growing larger; the day is almost gone. As the sun is about to set, I know I will be asked to leave the monastery and Gael is anxiously awaiting my arrival below.

The Abba straightens his tall, lean body and disappears into the Holy of Holies. He returns empty-handed, having restored the Book of Zadok to its rightful place in the Scripture oratory.

"Pastor Jeff, it is now time for you to leave our mountain sanctuary." He must have noticed the look of concern on my face and explains, "All visitors must leave the monastery at dusk."

"I know that," I reply impatiently.

"Is something wrong, Jeff?" he inquires.

"Yes!" I raise my voice. "What about the Book of Zadok?"

"What about the book?" he asks.

"Well, there's so much to it—the history, the wisdom, the intimate view of King Solomon's life, and the power of the story. . ."

The Abba remains silent for a moment, then meets my comment with a question. "Yes, what are you trying to tell me, Jeff?"

"I want to study this book. I would like to spend more time with it and digest its insights for my life." I hesitated and then brazenly asked, "Can I get a copy of this book? I would like to acquire the story so I might study it and share it with others."

"Jeff, Jeff, it is not possible," the Abba replies. "This is the rightful home for the book. It will not be removed. It must not be removed."

"Then why did you read it to me if you knew I couldn't keep it and use it in some way?" I could no longer hide my disappointment.

The Abba stands before me with his hands at his side, holding my gaze in his warm brown eyes. "I read it to bless you," he says softly.

Ignoring his thoughtful response, I continue bartering as if in the marketplace. "How am I to be blessed in wisdom and share it if I can't keep a copy?"

"Don't misunderstand me, Jeff. I did not say you could not keep the Book of Zadok."

"But you said—"

"I know what I said. You do not understand. You are not listening. Allow me to tell you plainly. The only way to keep the book and take it off the mountain is to carry it in your heart as a Gift."

His truthful words arrest me. As I consider his statement, I know he is right. I also know I didn't like it, but I could do nothing about it. I realize at that very moment I am ungratefully pushing the limits of my host and his beautiful, grace-filled hospitality. I look into his kind eyes and apologize.

"Please forgive my disrespect and lack of trust. Help me receive this Gift and carry it in my heart."

The Abba reaches over, touches his cross to my forehead, places his hand on my shoulder, and recites the following blessing:

God bless you,
God make your heart bright,
Go home in peace
In the name of Christ.

He then insists, "It is now time for you to go." Our eyes meet for the last time. We smile and embrace. I turn, leaving the sanctuary to take the trail to the gate and the rope. As I make my way down to the gate, I feel conflicted. Part of me wants to stay in order to learn more, but how could I do that? The other part wants to go and tell of my experience, but what could I say? Neither my thoughts nor my feelings are seasoned to maturity; they are displaced, bouncing all over within me. I need time to let it all sink in.

The priests are waiting for me at the gate, ready to help with my descent so they can close the gate for the evening. As I grasp the precarious rope, I am acutely aware of earth's gravitational pull. Descending too quickly or carelessly would risk serious injury, even death. I also notice the weight of spiritual gravity drawing me downward. I am amazed and thankful for the wonder of my day at this mountain sanctuary. During this brief moment of reflection, while I'm suspended on the rope between two worlds, I feel cocooned by the peace and care holding me. Yet, the mass of both physical and spiritual gravity conspire to interrupt my reflection.

As my feet inch closer to the ground, my mind is overtaken by a plague of questions: *Will I return to my lonely, anxious burdens? Will I become consumed by urgency and overwhelmed by the busyness of life down below? Will I indeed carry the blessing I received in my own heart? Could I share the Gift with others? And how would I do this?*

At the bottom of the rope, Gael and our driver, Misganu, are waiting. As we walk to the Land Cruiser, we can hear the faint sound of the bell— the monks' call to evening prayer—over our shoulders. I simply receive its peaceful benediction, resisting the temptation to look back. We drive in silence under an ever darkening African sky toward the holy city of Axum.

The next day as we are preparing to leave Ethiopia for home, my mind keeps thinking about that extraordinary day at Debre Damo. I had an amazing experience with the monks, the Abba, and the Book of Zadok. All of this was due, in part, to that curious encounter with the guardian of the Ark in Axum. I considered once again, as I had on the mountaintop, *Was all this simply a remarkable coincidence? Or had it been of divine origin? If so, what purpose could this serve?* I realized my many questions and fanciful imagination would keep me wondering for a very long time. At this point, I had to concede, I knew nothing for sure. However, each time I would recall the events of that most unusual day, it would seem more and more like some kind of fascinating dream.

✠

The Seven Secrets
Hidden in Plain Sight

Upon my return from Ethiopia, I was pursued by the memories of my experience. Haunted might be too strong a word to describe what I felt. Just the same, its presence followed me everywhere. At first I attempted to sort it out through reason: *What could I recall? How did it happen? Who was involved? And why?* This line of questioning proved exhausting and pointless, leading me nowhere.

My heart charted an alternative course of inquiry, moving away from the causal toward the essence: *What had I noticed? How was I moved? What did I feel? What insights have I continued to wonder about?* These questions produced a ripe harvest of spiritual wisdom.

You see, having heard the unique story of Solomon, I was curiously drawn to the transparent rendering of the king's spiritual crisis. This observation has given rise to three realizations. First, I noticed that Solomon wrestled with what we moderns have identified as the classic struggle between our true and false selves. In fact, according to Zadok this was the epic battle of his spiritual life. Perhaps it was his life.

Second, I have come to recognize that I too can relate to the king's spiritual dilemma. I identify and am well acquainted with this quandary of my own true and false self. Finally, I have found myself uncomfortably wondering about the spiritual terms "true and false self." I believe I understand their intended meaning and purpose. However, I also sense that they don't quite fit for me; they leave me feeling confused, unfulfilled, and wanting.

Having considered this last observation, I've concluded that the words true and false suggest an overstated and extremely severe dichotomy. They seem to divide, tearing me apart rather than pulling me together. Unfortunately, this wording creates an unnecessary wall of separation rather than a pathway of growth. Even so, I have become attracted to the words "whole and broken self." The language of whole and broken opens a doorway of healing for me, gently taking my broken self by the hand and patiently leading me toward wholeness.

Like a bridge between two major gaps in my life, I can now envision the road spreading out before me, encouraging and inviting me. Similar to King Solomon, I am learning to embrace my whole and broken self as a lifelong exercise.

Therefore I recognize that my whole self is the authentic and unique person God has created me to be. God has designed and shaped me to fulfill my spiritual destiny for which I was created in the image of God. This is by no means a perfect self or a life with no pain, difficulties, or mishaps. However, through my whole self I can experience a complete, vital, and fulfilled life in the midst of suffering, hardship, joy, and hope.

Conversely, my broken self is also present. It draws me away from my whole self, tempting me to sinful selfishness and destructive behavior. The lure of my broken self appeals to my conceited sense of entitlement (I deserve it), my need for control (only I can do it right), and my desire for instant gratification (I want it now!). These temptations are spoken to me in words that are attractive but deceptive: "Jeff, take this shortcut, and you'll have more of what you want and sooner. You'll even get to do it all yourself, *your* way." It always sounds good, but when I go for it, I'm never successful nor satisfied.

Frustrated, desperate, and fearful that my carefully managed life is slipping away, my broken self is prepared to ambush me with a new temptation. This one is more insidious than the last, yet very common. "Jeff, if your shortcuts aren't working, why don't you place a mask over them to hide your problems and simply appear like you want. Just act the part." This too is enticing and can even work for awhile, yet it too ultimately comes undone, leaving me frustrated and discontented. When my outward appearance exceeds my inward disposition, my life falls apart, unraveling from the inside out.

My whole self, God's blueprint for my life, can repel the temptations of the broken self. However, I must honestly accept the presence of my broken self, whose wayward force leaves me spiritually dislocated. Only then am I free to embrace my whole self by turning to God, who realigns my life. This process is akin to remembering all that has been dismembered within me.

I continue to feel the diminishing presence of my counterfeit self rise up whenever I attempt to fulfill some need by my own strength. However, I also sense God's growing presence gently, patiently, and compassionately reminding me, "Jeff, receive yourself through Me; you can't find it or create it on your own. Turn to Me, accept my Gift for you."

This is the very struggle I recognized and was drawn to in the life of Solomon. Becoming a witness to the king's spiritual issues in the Book of Zadok has compelled me to be aware of the same tensions in my own life. Perhaps the Abba sensed this resemblance between us and therefore chose to read me the king's story.

Over the years, I have summarized my thoughts and notes, organizing them in a style similar to Solomon's last lecture. I have interpreted Solomon's wisdom, applying it to my life and context. I continue to use these notes as a guide for my own spiritual examen and discernment. Even though I originally and specifically addressed these notes to myself, I now invite you to these reflections for your own consideration.

A final thought . . . Solomon used an architectural metaphor in his summary most likely because he was a builder—"the seven pillars." I have borrowed a contemporary metaphor from Parker Palmer as it speaks to my heart's longing and search for wisdom: "The Seven Secrets Hidden in Plain Sight."

As a result of my experience, I am learning seven life secrets.

They have remained a mystery in every generation by a peculiar means; these very important secrets are hidden in plain sight. By this I mean I can walk right past these secrets in everyday life without even noticing them. If I do notice, I often trample them underfoot as if they were fool's gold.

However, these secrets are genuine, indispensable treasures. When I refuse to recognize and acknowledge these secrets hidden in plain sight, I forfeit their spiritual benefits. Even when these secrets are counterintuitive to my natural ways of thinking, which is frequent, they remain essential if I desire to live a wise and vital life.

Secret #1: *Accept Yourself.*

Without self-acceptance, life becomes bitter and negative. I need to become comfortable in my own skin, receiving myself. I should be able to hold a mirror to my face, gaze into my own eyes, and smile. How am I to affirm others when I won't affirm myself? My critical judgment of others betrays my own inner critic and lack of self-acceptance.

Self-acceptance does not mean I overlook my problems and faults. It means unconditionally accepting both my whole and broken self as my complete self, learning from and living with both. In order to walk away from and resist the bondage of my broken self, I must first walk with it through acceptance. Refusing to do so, I am most vulnerable to becoming one of the following:

- A perfectionist obsessed with self-improvement. In doing so, I jump on the treadmill of self-realization, which keeps me busy but leads nowhere.

- A fatalist giving up on life, paralyzed by my own impossible expectations. In doing so, cynicism leaves its negative scent on everything I think, do, and say.

- An imposter, attempting to hide behind a mask. In doing so, what I hide from others gets buried deep inside, tangled in a web of self-deception.

Therefore, I will consider all of me as myself, not just the parts I like. I cannot allow my life to become a series of problems to be solved. Instead I will learn to accept all of who I am now, in order to become all I am going to be. I will remain rooted in the great commandment that declares that loving God and my neighbor is immutably linked to truly loving myself.

Secret #2: *Approach Change as an Opportunity*.

Change cannot be forced either from within (myself) or from the outside (others). I cannot make the difficult aspects of my life go away by sheer willpower or grim determination. Even when I've recognized a need for change, I often allow either fear or laziness to chase away my good intentions. Likewise, change imposed upon me will become change opposed by me. I notice my resistance rise when unsolicited advice comes my way.

I am encouraged that Secret #1 (Accept Yourself) opens the door to approaching change in a whole new way—as an opportunity rather than an obligation. When embracing myself, I recognize the broken areas of my life that long to be healed. When realizing my neediness, my good and noble qualities are also revealed. Being reminded of my good qualities lightens the heavy burden of facing my shortcomings, which enables me to approach change as a hopeful opportunity.

When I approach change as an opportunity, I am yielding to God's power for transformation. As long as I attempt to change myself, I remain in bondage to the fruitlessness of my own self-effort. In doing so, I block the powerful transforming hand of God. Whenever I let go of my own grip on change and grab God's outstretched hand, I am set free to receive God's transforming opportunities:

- The opportunity to admit to needed change.
- The opportunity to identify specific areas of change.
- The opportunity to acknowledge my fear of change.
- The opportunity to replace the broken life with a whole life.

As I trust in God, the opportunities do arise for me to choose a new attitude over an old one, a different thought over a former thought, and a change of approach to the same situation. The broken self recedes as the whole self proceeds to replace it. I am finding that change is never quick, so I'm learning to accept slow progress rather than expect overnight perfection.

Finally, two wonderful and necessary qualities keep me reaching for God's opportunity—honesty and humility. Honesty keeps me focused on God's ability and my inability to change. Humility frees me to accept my need, trusting and waiting on God's power for transformation.

Secret #3: *Embrace Failure and Difficulty as Teachers.*

Failure and difficulty have more to teach me about growth and maturity than success. I am a poor student of success, for I foolishly become conceited and forget about God. Failure and difficulties underscore my need, while presenting me with an opportunity to trust God. God uses my failure and difficulty to dismantle my broken self. It is through this deconstruction that my whole self is constructed. God desires that I grow from my mistakes rather than dwell on them. My hardships have much to teach me, as long as I am willing to listen and learn from them (or unlearn, as the case may be).

I can waste my whole life doing one of the following:

- Resent my disappointments.
- Complain about my misfortunes.
- Regard my circumstances as unmerited punishment.

However, when I yield to the above, I am not merely a victim of my trials, but I become a collaborator with them. God is not judging or punishing me but redeeming and transforming me.

The laws of nature reveal that the ground is nourished and made fruitful through fertilizing decay. Sorrow, due to decay in my life, will nourish and make me fruitful as well. Failure and difficulty, in reality, are strange allies disguised as enemies for my own good. When I accept trouble as a legitimate part of life, it leads me to God. When I depend on life meeting my expectations, I invite frustration and defeat. The test of my spiritual wisdom comes when I am confronted with turmoil, injustice, failure, and hurt. Will I quit, give way to self-pity, becoming bitter and angry; or will I turn to the only wise and true God?

I am learning that life centered upon God and wisdom is not easy, yet in time it will yield fruit such as peace, hope, joy, and love. Life apart from God and wisdom is a very lonely existence and barren of any vital, life-giving fruit. On days when I'm troubled and burdened, and I hear myself complaining, "When does all this bad stuff go away?" I eventually return to this surprising yet hopeful answer: "When I am thankful for it."

Secret #4: *Become a Compassionate Influence Using the Ears, Not the Tongue.*

The ability to listen, sufficient to understanding, has become important beyond all measure for myself and those around me. When I look at my face, I see I was made with two ears but only one tongue. This is not merely an anatomical fact; it illustrates where my true influence lies. I was made with more capacity to listen than to talk. However, I must admit I speak more than I listen. Often my talk is ill-informed because I have not taken the time to listen. When I listen, I invoke at least three blessings; I open myself to hear:

- God, with hope and trust,
- Others, with interest and affirmation,

- Myself, with appreciation for my own thoughts and feelings.

When I talk too much I am more likely to lean on my own understanding, allowing my broken self to inhabit my thoughts and words. In the stillness of listening, my whole self inclines to the words that I hear, granting me understanding. Misunderstanding and conflict stem primarily from inadequate listening. Being present with the following questions helps me yield to listening:

- What does the sound and intensity of my voice communicate about me?
- Do I hear what others are trying to say?
- Does what I hear inspire growth or defensiveness in me?
- Do people feel listened to around me?

I've discovered two unintended consequences of not listening. First, when I do not listen to another completely, I find them resistant to my comments, even when my responses are encouraging and helpful. Why? Because my lack of listening sends a painful message of rejection, underrating them as persons and undervaluing their stories. Everyone wants to feel like they are being heard.

Second, when I do not listen, I am resisting the person who needs to talk and the words they desire to share. My unwillingness to listen increases my chances of continued misunderstanding.

Becoming a wise listener may become the most important talent I could ever acquire from God. By deeply listening to another person (not merely their words), I will be offering influence, insight, and encouragement that goes beyond words.

Secret #5: *Receive the Wisdom That Comes Through Obedience.*

Spiritual wisdom comes through obedience. Not simply what I know, but what I do with what I know, is wisdom. Obedience applies what I know to what I do and makes me wise. Sadly, I currently know more than I'm willing to obey, which often makes me foolish. However, I have hope in realizing that true wisdom is in obedience rather than knowledge.

God imparts wisdom not so I can look and feel clever, but so I will become wise. When I disobey God, I block wisdom's flow. God offers wisdom on a single condition—that I use it.

Signs of obedience that lead to wisdom:

- Obedience for obedience's sake is neither virtuous nor wise; instead, it is foolish.
- Obedience-producing wisdom occurs in response to God.
- Every time I obey, God is encouraging, empowering, and leading me with greater wisdom.
- Obeying God's plans often upsets all other plans—including my own.
- Obedience allows me to participate in the essential generosity and wisdom of God, rather than my essential selfishness apart from God.
- Obedience yields to the wisdom of God, allowing me to receive it and pass it on to others.

My daily need for wisdom and God's faithful supply builds an amazing love and trust relationship between us. Trusting in God, I am weaned from obeying the dictates of my broken foolishness. Obeying God, I receive my whole self through the wisdom that God imparts.

Secret #6: *Apply Wisdom to Others—Love.*

Just as the first secret reminds me of the importance of healthy love of self and the seventh secret will affirm my necessity to love God above all else, the sixth secret directs my attention to loving others. When I do not love others, I cast a shadow of doubt over truly loving myself or God.

Loving myself and God takes place primarily deep in my heart.

However, when this interior love is insufficient, it manifests its short-coming in my exterior relationships as a lack of love towards others. How I treat others (especially the most difficult people) is an incredibly accurate measure of the fullness or absence of love in my life. Therefore, I seek to be aware of the following harmful characteristics when they are present in my life:

- Am I impatient with or overly critical of others?
- Do I think of others in ways I would dare not speak out loud?
- Do I find myself suspicious of others, considering them untrustworthy?
- Do I hold high expectations or standards over others?
- Am I particularly skillful at finding others' faults?

On the one hand, I have considered that God knows everything about everyone and chooses to respond to all people with love, including me. On the other hand, I notice I pick and choose whom I love. I make my assessment of others, and love or withhold accordingly.

God seeks to show the way of wisdom through loving me unconditionally. God longs for me to love others as I have been loved. What would happen if I love others as God loves me? It's a powerful, hopeful, and worthy meditation. God's love:

- Welcomes and encourages me. Am I welcoming?
- Shows me undeserved mercy. What do I show?
- Gracefully allows me to be myself. Do I grant others their originality?
- Generously gives me second chances. Do I freely offer the same?
- Completely forgives me. How thorough is my pardon?

As it turns out, God's love for me is incredible. God receives all my imperfections and is carefully and patiently transforming them. As I begin to love others as God has loved me, my broken self shrinks while my whole self expands. My critical and inhospitable behavior towards others is being replaced by the wisdom of loving others.

Secret #7: *Love the Giver Not Just the Gift.*

I confess continued distraction as I grow in spiritual maturity and wisdom, neglecting God for the Gift. I willingly love God's gifts without loving God, the Giver.

Driven by my brokenness, fears, and insecurities, I pursue my needs in an attempt to fix myself. However, at the end of my failed striving and futile attempts, I again meet God's loving presence. When I give up trying to do God's job, I find God lovingly working on my behalf.

A holy thread of hope weaves through all seven secrets—God's love for me. God always loves me and has my best interests in mind even when it doesn't seem or feel like it. God's love for me is the sacred fire of divine romance. God's love is continuously courting me, wooing me to an ever growing, ever deepening relationship. What I find even more astonishing is that I am not only invited to inhabit God's love, but I am also given the means to return that love as well. As I experience the sacred fire of God's love, I am filled to overflowing with love towards God.

All this begs the question: How am I to love God? What have I to give? God longs for one thing from me, the only thing I am able to give—myself. God desires that I offer myself in this sacred fire of love. I am seeking to do this in the following active prayers:

O Lord, I offer you:
- My right to myself; enable me to put You first in everything.
- My gifts and abilities, to use or not as You will and desire.
- My weakness, asking for Your help and strength in my need.
- My faith, believing that You are in control of everything.
- My fears, trusting You in the darkness and uncertainty of life.
- My success, giving You glory for everything.

- My sin, receiving Your mercy and forgiveness.
- My worship; You are worthy of all praise and honor.

The offering of my very self is loving God with all my heart, soul, mind, and strength. Loving God first, I truly begin to love others and myself. In this sacred fire of love my broken self is consumed and my whole self is forged. My focus is trained on the Giver and not merely the gift. This is the way of wisdom and the purpose of life.

The seven secrets have no power to make me wise or transform my life, just as the Gift in Solomon's hands was in itself useless. God is the one who transforms me and leads me to wisdom. The secrets, however, are God's tools leading me to transformation. Attending to the secrets will open my heart and prepare me, so I will neither miss nor misunderstand God's way.

For the secrets to be generative in my life, they cannot become an end in themselves. They must lead me into the presence of God. In God's faithful presence I neither lose heart when things go terribly wrong, nor lose my head when things go wonderfully well. Even losing sight of God offers me the unexpected blessing of being sought after by the shepherd of my soul. Therefore, I choose to place my hope in God's faithfulness to patiently find me, love me, transform me, and bless me in the way of wisdom.

To the best of my ability I have attempted to relate my experience and have committed to writing that which I received on that holy mountain in Ethiopia. I invite you to be with the Gift, let your life become enlarged and transformed, blessing those you meet along your journey. —Jeff

BOOK NOTES

The biblical story of King Solomon is found in 1 Kings, chapters 1-11 and 2 Chronicles, chapters 1-9. Books of the Bible attributed to Solomon include: most, but not all, of Proverbs and the book of Ecclesiastes.

The original idea for the Gift as a window and mirror came from a leadership illustration used by Jim Collins in his book *Good to Great*.

The story of the five birds, thoughts on intention and mistakes (chapter 19), came from motivational speaker and writer Andy Andrews in his book *The Noticer*.

The spirituality quote attributed to the wise Rabbi (chapter 16), the Sufi story adapted to King Solomon, challenging a loving God (chapter 18), and the often told Hasidic Zusya story adapted to King Solomon's dream (chapter 23) all came from the wonderful book, *The Spirituality of Imperfection: Storytelling and the Search for Meaning* by Ernest Kurtz and Katherine Ketcham.

Insight relating to self-acceptance, difficulty, and failure (chapter 20) I attribute to Parker J. Palmer, specifically in his books: *The Active Life* and *Let Your Life Speak*. The concept of life secrets hidden in plain sight (chapter 20) was gleaned from *A Hidden Wholeness* also by Parker J. Palmer.

Three books deserve mention for historical research and background context: *Ethiopia* by Mohamed Amin and Duncan Willetts, *Ethiopia Travel Guide* by Philips Briggs, and *Black Angels: the Art and Spirituality of Ethiopia* by Richard Marsh.

The classic devotional *My Utmost for His Highest* by Oswald Chambers was influential throughout the book, especially in the area of obedience (chapter 20). Likewise, *One Day at a Time in Al-Anon* finds its way into this story often.

The engaging and stirring music from Bob Bennett's *Small Graces* and *Song's From Bright Avenue* have been most inspirational. Lyrics from these compact discs have seasoned the text of this story.

ENDNOTES

i Psalm 139:23-24 (NASB)

ii Exodus 34:5-7

iii 1 Kings 3:5-14

iv 1 Kings 3:14

v Psalm 51:1-19

vi 2 Kings 2:2-4

vii Psalm 46:10

viii Numbers 33:2

ix Proverbs 2:1-6

x Proverbs 4:7-9

xi Proverbs 14:33

xii Proverbs 3:5-6

xiii Psalm 139:23-24

xiv 1 Kings 3:16-28

xv 1 Kings 8:23-30, 52

xvi 1 Kings 4:33-34

xvii 1 Kings 10:6-9

xviii 1 Kings 10:13

xix 1 Kings 10:23-24

xx Proverbs 15:13

xxi Proverbs 21:1-2

xxii Proverbs 23:12, 15-16

xxiii Proverbs 27:19

xxiv Proverbs 7:1-3

xxv Luke 10:27

About the Author

Jeff Mitchell is a pastor and spiritual director who resides in Valley Springs, California, with his wife, Gael. Jeff occasionally leads retreats and is a conference speaker and teacher.

Note: A seven session study guide based on Solomon's Seven Pillars (Chap. 18) and the author's Seven Secrets is available on the website.

You may contact Jeff Mitchell through the following means:

Good Samaritan Community Covenant Church
4684 Baldwin Street
Valley Springs, CA 95252
Tel (209) 772-9548   Fax (209) 772-0451

Email: gsccc@wildblue.net
Website: www.jeffmitchelltakingheart.com